MURDER—HIS & HERS: STORIES

MAX ALLAN COLLINS
AND
BARBARA COLLINS

WOLFPACK
PUBLISHING
— EST 2013 —

MURDER—HIS & HERS: STORIES

For our moms

Contents

Intro/His: Max Allan Collins

I share with my wife a love for the twist ending, and I suppose our short stories tend to be a little old-fashioned . . . though in a good way.

Recently I co-edited (with Jeff Gelb) a collection of short stories *(Flesh and Blood)* that included a cross-section of writers in the mystery/suspense genre, from old pros to young punks. I liked all of the stories—or I wouldn't have bought them!—but several stood out. Writers like Ed Hoch and Don Westlake (to name just two longtime professionals who contributed to that anthology) crafted the kind of well-made story we don't see much these days. Every nut, every bolt, in its proper place, every screw turn of the plot perfectly tightened . . . with a final pay-off that provided a smile, or a tingle at the back of the neck ... or both.

These days, we see some very interesting stories—unusual ones, daring ones, rule- and ground-breakers. But we rarely see the kind of perfectly fashioned story that used to be, well, fairly commonplace in our popular culture. The great weekly "slick" magazines—*Saturday Evening Post* and *Collier's* come to mind—and the wonderful pulps—*Black Mask* anyone?— are long gone; so are the half-hour radio and TV dramas. I grew up on *Tales from the Crypt* and other great comic books (mostly EC's); and—while HBO mined those ancient ghoulish funnies for several seasons a while back—those are long gone, too.

This makes the short story a sort of lost art. A lot of the short stories written today—many of them good, even terrific—are the work of novelists . . . like me . . . taking an occasional dip into the short-fiction pool, at the invite of the editor of an anthology, or to take a crack at the few remaining markets, like *Ellery Queen's Mystery Magazine* and *Alfred Hitchcock's Mystery Magazine.* Some top-notch novelists— like John Lutz, Ed Gorman and Lawrence Block—are also first-rate short story writers; and I like to think I'm not bad at it myself, if not in the league of those mentioned.

But I'm not a born short story writer. I think in complicated, complex ways that make for a good novel, and it's difficult for me to work in miniature. My wife, Barb—who is swiftly becoming a skilled novelist, by the way—has a knack for precision work. You'll see examples of that in the pages ahead.

Now and then we write a story together (we always help each other on individual projects) and we've never had a problem, none of the expected marital battles. Perhaps she's just used to dealing with my bloated, fragile ego. Or maybe it's just that we stay out of each other's way, after we come up with a plot in a story conference over lunch or on a Sunday afternoon drive—she writes her draft, and I write mine.

Now and then we trade off sections. There's more of me in the Sam Knight voice in "Eddie Haskell in a Short Skirt," and more of Barb in Rebecca's. She is notorious, in our collaborations, for leaving me dangling: in the middle of a beautifully crafted sequence, in which I'm all caught up as a reader, I will encounter FIGHT SCENE HERE.

Anyway, we work well together—and we do well on our own. We hope you'll find the tales in this collection—whether hers, mine or ours—worthy examples of the almost lost art of the well-made tale with a twist of wry.

Intro /Hers: Barbara Collins

Back in the 1950s, when there were only a few TV channels to watch, three shows brought to a screeching halt the mayhem in the kid-infested house I grew up in: *Perry Mason* (my mother had a mad crush on Raymond Burr), *Maverick* (my mother had a mad crush on James Garner), and *Alfred Hitchcock Presents* (my mother did *not* have a mad crush on the great director, but loved the stories). These programs must have had a profound effect on me, because the key ingredients of each episode—mystery, humor, irony—seem to make up the recipe I follow for my own short stories.

Even though I have worked in the novel format, to me, the perfect way to tell a tale is the short story. It's great for impatient people with short attention spans, one of which I am. And my husband, who encouraged me to write and has been a great teacher, has always touted, "Write what *you 'd* like to read."

Some of my favorite stories are ones that we've collaborated on; it's a little bit me, a little bit him. Having a male/female perspective is always interesting. And our writing styles are so similar (no surprise) that, come the end result, even we sometimes can't tell who wrote what.

Besides my husband—who is one of the smartest, best writers in the whole wide world—I owe a debt of gratitude to Ed Gorman and Marty Greenberg for publishing my stories in their wonderful anthologies.

Another debt is owed, of course. The stories in this book are sometimes by me, sometimes by my husband, sometimes by the two of us, working together. But the most important collaborator, in any story, is the reader. We've done our job—the rest is up to you!

Eddie Haskell in a Short Skirt

The Polk County Prison was located just north of Des
Moines on four well-manicured acres. The newly
constructed twenty-million dollar complex had no
unsightly barbed wire fence surrounding its premises,
nor a guard station at the front entry, or anything else
that made it look like a prison. To the passer-by, the
two-story red brick octagonal building might have
been a clinic of some kind, a place you might go to
have a skin tag lopped off, or an impacted molar ex-
tracted. Only the back of the building gave its purpose
away: rows of small barred windows ran its length,
windows so tiny that a man—or woman—couldn't
possibly squeeze through.

    I'd been to this prison just one other time, with my
father, Sam Knight, to visit a client. He and I—my
name is Rebecca—are partners in an investigations

firm in the city. (You might have read about us in *People* magazine last year for cracking "The Cutthroat Cowgirl Case"—their title, not ours.)

Getting back to the prison, I was really impressed by this state-of-the-art facility, with its laser sensors, computer-operated doors, and prisoner tracking bracelets. Even the cells were fairly comfortable, clean and new.

Anyway, mine was.

I was in for murdering my best friend, Vickie.

Footsteps echoed down the concrete hallway coming toward me, sounding like pop-guns going off, but I remained motionless on the little bed, my hands clenched tightly in my lap. Then a deputy sheriff, tall and gangly, was punching in numbers on a security pad, opening the barred door, informing me my father was here.

In the visitation room, which was small but not claustrophobic, my father and I sat at a long table, the width of which was between us. He looked older than his sixty-four years, older than I'd ever seen him, his craggy face drawn, bronze tan faded from the long winter months. But his eyes were strong, determined. If he was at all frightened, those ol' blue eyes did not betray him.

I, too, must have looked a sight: no make-up, shoulder length brown hair uncombed, and very un-fashionable in the orange prison dress with orange slip-on tennies.

He cleared his throat. "Are they treating you

okay, pumpkin?" He'd hardly called me that since grade school.

I nodded numbly.

"Got a call in to Walter Conlon," he told me. "He's a good criminal lawyer."

I nodded again. I would need the best.

Now my father stood up and came around the side of the table to stand before me, running the fingers of one hand on the table top, looking down at that hand. His voice was soft, even gentle. "You understand bail won't even be an issue until you've been arraigned."

"I understand," I said weakly.

I stood up and gave him the bravest smile I could muster, which wasn't much of one. "I'll be all right in here, really."

Then I fell into his arms, like I promised myself I wouldn't do, reduced from age thirty-four to four, and sobbed into his chest, leaving big, wet stains on his gray suit jacket, crying for me, crying for Vickie.

He smoothed my hair and said, "I could stay here longer if you want, but I'd like to get right to work on this."

"What is there you can do?"

He gave me a funny smile. "I might think of something. You hang in there, pumpkin."

Back in my cell, I returned to the bed, where I sat staring at the tan wall.

If only I hadn't gone to The Brew that night, our paths wouldn't have crossed. . . And I wouldn't be sitting here now with my life and business in shambles.

But then, our meeting again after so many years hadn't really been left to chance, had it? Because Vickie had come to town looking for me. I realized that now, too late.

We'd met in the seventh grade, Vickie and me, and soon became good friends. I had a cousin, Ann, a few years older, who'd had a number of best friends in school. One by one they betrayed her: Sue spread nasty, false rumors; Janice stole her boyfriend, and Liz got her kicked off the Pom-Pom squad when Ann gained a few pounds. I watched on the sidelines and made up my mind not ever to have a best friend.

But the more time I spent with Vickie, the more she seemed like the genuine thing: someone I could confide in and trust. She knew the value of keeping secrets. Hadn't she given me my first diary, for my thirteenth birthday?

And she was so confident, out-going and fun. Qualities I felt I lacked. When I was around her, she made me feel like a different person, a person I liked much better.

I lost track of Vickie after high school, when we went on to different colleges, me to the University of Minnesota, her to Northwestern. She didn't come back for our tenth high school reunion, but a photo of her (looking gorgeous behind a desk in a fancy high-rise office) was tacked on the bulletin board, along with those of other classmates who couldn't make it back. An accompanying letter said she and a partner named Kyle owned a very successful insurance company in Chicago. A p.s. on the note said, "A special hello to Rebecca!"

So you can imagine my surprise and delight when I turned around from the bar at The Brew six months ago, a glass of Chablis in one hand, to see my old friend Vickie. We squealed like little pigs, and hugged, and laughed and hugged some more, then found a booth in the back.

"You look terrific," I told Vickie. And she did: long blond hair, startlingly blue eyes, porcelain skin, perfect white teeth. "Don't have a portrait of yourself, getting wrinkled in the attic, do you?" I asked.

She laughed and shook her head. "You look wonderful, too," she said.

Maybe. Maybe not. But it was nice of her to say it.

"What brings you back to town?" I asked.

"I'm going to open my own insurance agency here," she said happily.

"Really!" I was thrilled. I reached out and squeezed her hand, immediately visualizing us lunching at Noah's, shopping at Valley Junction, and spending Friday evenings at Billy Joe's Pitcher Show. Just like the good old days.

She ran one manicured fingernail around the rim of the glass of red wine she'd brought to the table, and looked down into the drink. "But before I can," she said, "I have to pass the Iowa exam, since I'm only licensed in Illinois. But that shouldn't be too hard."

Not for her. "What happened to your other insurance business?" I asked.

Her face clouded, and she stared off into the smoky, noisy room behind us. "My partner—Kyle was his name—and I had a rather bad falling out."

"I'm sorry."

She took a sip of her drink. "It's not what you think . . . We weren't lovers or anything. Just business partners who couldn't see eye to eye."

"I understand." I'd been there with my father, but never bad enough to call it quits.

"I couldn't take his unethical practices anymore," she explained sadly.

Curious, I asked, "What do you mean by 'unethical practices'?"

She paused a moment, wineglass to her lips. "Kyle would give customers more coverage than they needed, with outrageously high premiums, just so he could collect a big commission." She took a sip of wine, then added, "That's just one example, and believe me, there were plenty of others."

"Wow." I'd read about such scurrilous practices that were rampant in the 1980s, when suddenly, reputable insurance corporations found themselves in legal hot water because of some unethical agents. It cost the corporations millions and millions to settle all the claims.

"I just had to get out," Vickie said, pain showing on her pretty face, "so I left it all behind."

I smiled supportively at her. That must have been hard. That must have taken guts.

"Anyway," she went on, "the first thing I have to

do is find a temporary job, until I can move forward with my plans. Got any ideas?"

And a bolt of lightning struck me. Three weeks ago I let our office manager go because of poor performance, and I hadn't gotten around to finding a replacement, doing the work myself.

"Have I!" I said. "You can come and work for me, doing bookkeeping and such."

"Really?" she asked, her face lighting up. Then she sat back in the booth, putting one hand to her forehead, like she felt faint. "Oh, Reb, I'm soooo embarrassed. Here I've been talking about myself and my problems, never once asking you about yourself."

"That's all right," I said, warmed by how considerate she was. "I run an investigations firm here in the city. With my father."

"No kidding?" she said. "How exciting. With your father, you say."

"Uh-huh."

"How is he? Did he ever remarry after your mom died?"

"Nope. Too set in his ways."

She gave me a half-smile. "I always thought you were so lucky having him for a dad."

I smiled back; such a nice thing of her to say.

We fell silent for a few seconds, then Vickie raised her glass. "Here's to us," she said.

Our glasses clinked together. And I downed my drink.

Vickie would be perfect for the job, I had thought. After all, she had a business degree. She couldn't possibly do any worse than the previous manager had done.

You think you're way out in front of me, don't you?

Well, within a week Vickie had cleaned up the mess left by the other manager—straightening out the payroll, collecting delinquent accounts receivable, even cracking down on employee pilfering of company supplies. She ran one hell of a tight ship with, "Do we really need that?" and "Can't we buy it cheaper?"

Within the next few months, the coffers at Knight and Knight and Associates had never looked fuller. Which, in hindsight, made a lot of sense. Because there was just that much more money for her to steal.

Which she did.

Yesterday, Friday, the first day of Spring, I stayed late at the office to finish some paperwork when I got a call from a west coast electronics firm we'd purchased some surveillance gear from, saying their bill was ninety days overdue. I assured them there must be some kind of mistake because we always pay on time, but I'd look into it and call them back Monday morning.

I went into Vickie's office to scribble her a note about checking on the overdue bill, and I opened the right hand desk drawer looking for a note-pad. There was the company checkbook, so I flipped back through the register and found that the check to the LA firm had been written nearly a month ago. But there was no check mark by it, which meant that it hadn't cleared—as hadn't a great many of the checks written two, even three, months ago.

Some checks *had* cleared—ones written every week for thousands of dollars, payable to Vickie and marked "expenses."

Only we'd given Vickie no expense account privilege.

Ten minutes later, I found a large manila envelope stuffed in the back of the bottom drawer of a file cabinet; it contained the bills and checks that she'd never mailed.

It's hard to describe how I felt that moment, but anyone who's ever been betrayed by someone they trust knows. The range of emotions was incredible: shock, disbelief, sadness.

Rage.

I don't remember getting my gun out of the safe in my office, but I must have, because I had it in my hand as I stood outside Vickie's apartment on Hickman Road, using the butt of it to bang on her door as I called her bad names.

I knew she was home because her car was in the lot. So when she didn't answer I shot wildly at the wooden door, the third bullet taking the knob off, then shouldered it open.

She was sprawled on the floor by the front door, facedown, wearing the same blue suit she'd had on at work; a puddle of blood spread out from her chest like a red fan, soaking the beige carpet. She must have been coming to answer the door, I realized, when she was struck by one of my bullets.

Behind me, in the hallway, I heard alarmed voices. Someone yelled to call 911. My legs felt rubbery and I stepped into the apartment and eased myself into a chair by the front door to wait for the police to come. I felt detached, strangely cold—an out of body experience.

The room was in disarray, with papers and magazines strewn about and cardboard boxes sitting half-filled. On a coffee table lay Vickie's purse, open, its contents dumped out. And next to the table were two large black suitcases, ready to go.

I remember thinking that it wasn't very nice of Vickie to leave the apartment in such a mess.

It just wasn't very nice at all.

The only thing harder than seeing my little girl sitting in that prison was leaving her there. But if I'd stayed any longer, she'd have got wind of how scared I was.

The Chief of Police had tracked me down the night before at Barney's Pub where I was watching ESPN on a big screen, pretending an O'Doul's was a real beer (I'm a recovering alcoholic). At first I thought he was joking about the trouble Becky was in, because she's so straight it's embarrassing, and the Chief has a sense of humor like a rash.

But there was too much sadness in those rheumy eyes.

I know my daughter's got a temper—you can blame my gene pool—because I've seen it once or twice, and it's not a pretty thing. But I never thought she'd get mad enough to kill somebody. Especially her close friend Vickie.

I never liked that girl, from the first time she and Becky hooked up as kids; especially since that time I caught her reading Becky's diary. But I didn't let on. Becky seemed happy being around her, and as long as they weren't getting into trouble (none that I knew of, anyway), who was I to tell Becky who her friends should be. Most of mine, at the time, were fellow boozehounds.

But I'll tell you, I didn't like the way Becky behaved after spending time with Vickie, which was snotty and disrespectful.

So what was wrong with Vickie? She was smart, charming and pretty. Usually a good combination. Yet there was something phony about her. When she came over to the house, I felt like I was Ward Cleaver and she was Eddie Haskell in a short skirt.

And she used Becky. Used her homework, her clothes, her meager allowance, all the while playing the grateful friend. Which kept Becky giving her more.

Then there was the time Vickie stayed over when she was fourteen. In the middle of the night, I felt something soft and warm in my bed. She'd crawled under the covers and was crying about having a nightmare. I wasn't too sympathetic, though, thinking about another nightmare that might unfold if I didn't get her out of there. For years I believed it was just my dirty old man's mind that thought the worst of her

. . . until three weeks ago.

She showed up on the stoop of my bungalow a little toasty, looking mighty fetching in a tight, low-cut red dress. She had a wicker basket and in it was a bottle of wine and two glasses.

"Well," I said as I stood in the doorway, in a white undershirt and wrinkled trousers; I'd been watching a boxing match on the tube.

"This is quite a surprise. "She smiled seductively, looking up at me through veiled blue eyes. "Aren't you going to ask me in?"

I smiled back a little. "I don't think that would be a good idea," I said.

"What's the matter?" she teased. "I won't bite."

She had the basket, so why did I feel like Little Red Riding Hood and she was the Big Bad Wolf?

She shifted the basket in front of herself, holding it with both hands, swinging it from side to side as she twisted her body back and forth like Baby Snooks in an old Warner Brothers picture. "Besides," she said slyly, "I'm a little older than fourteen now. You don't have to be afraid."

I dropped my smile, feeling heat spreading across my cheeks, which doesn't happen very often. "I don't sleep with employees," I told her. "Clients, maybe—but never employees."

The sweet, seductive look on her face turned savage. "You son of a bitch!" she spat. "Why I thought to waste a good bottle of wine on an old dinosaur like you, I'll never know."

I did. "Maybe I'm the one thing of Becky's you never got your mitts on," I said.

And I shut the door in her face.

It wasn't easy sending her packing. But nobody likes being had, even in the most pleasant of ways.

I could have been wrong. Maybe it *was* possible for a thirty-year-old woman with an angel's face and a hell of a body to be attracted to a sixty-year-old man with a potbelly and a butch haircut.

And maybe one little drink wouldn't hurt, anyway. But I wasn't about to partake of either.

Night was settling in over the city as I wheeled my three-year-old Escort into the underground parking lot of 801 Grand, the deco marble tombstone of a building where we had our offices. I took the elevator up to the main lobby, which was deserted on this Saturday evening, and switched elevators up to the twenty-first floor.

A couple of things had been bothering me about the body and crime scene, which Chief Coderoni was kind enough to let me in to see. First, the blood left in Vickie's body, that which hadn't spilled out on the carpet, anyway, had just begun to discolor the skin and settle, which told me death was a little further along than it should be. I was willing to bet ballistics would find that the bullet didn't come from Becky's gun.

Second, while it made sense Vickie was in a hurry to vacate the apartment, the place just didn't look right. Drawers and cabinets hung open, but nothing seemed to have been removed. And the only time I'd ever seen my wife (rest her soul) dump the contents of her purse out, was when she was frustratedly looking for something. Whoever killed Vickie hadn't found what he—or she—was looking for.

Maybe that person was now looking elsewhere. The bronze elevator doors slid open and I stepped out into the hallway and followed the carpeted corridor around to the right, to the double glass doors of our office. I dug out my security card and used it to enter.

The reception area was dark, but the door leading into the back yawned open; I went quietly through it and into the bullpen area, which was awash in street-light and neon. Down a hallway to the right was my office, and Becky's. To the left was Vickie's, the door shut, but light streamed from under it. And I doubted Vickie was in there.

I took my snubnose .38 from my jacket pocket, where I'd slipped it from the car's glove compartment where I kept it. As I moved forward, I could hear the slamming of file drawers from behind the door. Who-ever was in there must have used Vickie's security card, from her purse, to get into our office.

I opened the door quickly, the snubnose ready.

"It's Pinkerton who never closes," I told the thin, middle-aged man in an expensive tan suit, who stood behind the desk, its top covered with files. The man's hair, which matched the suit, was cut conservatively, parted at the side, with bangs brushing the top of gold wire-framed glasses, behind which beady brown eyes went wide at the sight of me, his hands frozen inside a file he was going through.

"I just want my personal files," he said, defensively.

I stepped inside the room, gun trained on him. "And what files might those be?" I asked.

His eyes narrowed to slits, and he dropped his hands down to his side.

"Vickie took *personal* papers of mine when she left Denver," he said. "I want them back."

Now I knew who he was: the unethical, untrustworthy Kyle I'd heard Becky mention.

And the person who killed Vickie.

"Put your hands in the air," I said, with a little gesture of the gun. And he did, but one of his hands held a silenced automatic, which must have been lying on the desk, hidden behind the stacks of file folders.

There was a *snick* and a bullet missed me by inches, and I dove for the floor, firing back awkwardly, missing him. He was heading toward the office door before I could haul myself up, and I wasn't up to playing grab-ass with somebody, so I reached out and snatched a hefty stapler off the desk and flung it at him, smacking him in the back of the skull, and he went down like an arcade target. Lights out.

I stood up, breathing heavily. From the look of the blood that was oozing out of his head, he was going to need a few stitches. He was coming around when I said, "Buddy, that's a nasty gash—I hope to hell you're insured."

As impressed as I was with the Polk County Prison, I was more impressed by the smell of the Iowa countryside outside its walls.

Ballistics proved what my father had suspected from the start: the bullet that killed Vickie did not come from my gun, but Kyle's, and the autopsy report showed the time of death to be earlier than when I arrived at her apartment in a red-hot rage.

Apparently, from statements made, and from what we were able to piece together, Kyle ran the shady insurance business with the full approval of Vickie. In fact, Kyle taught her everything she needed to know about how to swindle a customer. You might say he taught her too well. Because later, perhaps when the partnership began to sour, she started keeping files of damaging evidence on him, to be used later for blackmail.

That cost her her life. And nearly mine, and my father's.

Last week, I hired a new office manager. You can bet I did a comprehensive background check. As a matter of fact, in the interview I gave the poor bastard such a grilling, a big sweat stain formed around his neck. But he's working out fine. Just the same, every couple of weeks or so, I stay late at the office . . . and look through the checkbook and files.

The *Des Moines Register* ran an article on the embezzlement, and made me look like a sap, but Virginia Kafer from *People* (who wrote that terrific piece a year ago) did a follow-up story, focusing on the betrayal of a best friend, which I thought came out okay.

Anyway, a few days after that *People* magazine article appeared, I got a call at the office from Sheila, a woman I was friends with in college. She was in town from San Francisco on a business trip and wanted to get together for lunch and talk about old times. I told her I was busy.

Dead and Breakfast

Laura sat in the front on the rider's side of the white Transport minivan in the Holiday Inn parking lot, waiting for her husband to come out of the lobby.

In the back seat, their son, Andy—a dark-haired, round-faced, eleven-year-old boy with glasses—was hunched over, peering into the small screen of his Turbo Express, moving the expensive video toy back and forth in his hands to catch the last fading rays of the sun.

Even with the volume turned down, Laura could hear the frantic tune of the game he was playing: *Splatterhouse*—a particularly violent one she didn't approve of (and wouldn't have allowed her husband to buy for the boy, if *she'd* been along on that shopping trip). She mentally blocked the sound out, gazing toward the horizon at the picture-postcard sunset descending on lush green trees.

Wisconsin was a beautiful state, and the weather had been perfect; but now dark, threatening clouds were moving quickly in, bringing to an end a memorable summer-vacation day.

She spotted her husband, Pete, coming out of the lobby. He'd only been in there a minute or so . . . not very long.

It wasn't a good sign.

"We're in trouble," he said, after opening the van's door and sliding in behind the wheel. The brow of his ruggedly handsome face was furrowed.

"No room?" she asked.

"No room."

"Let's try another."

Pete turned toward her. "Honey," he said, his expression grave, "according to the desk clerk, there's not a vacancy between Milwaukee and Minneapolis."

"But that's impossible!" Laura said, astounded. "What's going on?"

Pete started the van. "A country festival, for one thing," he replied. "And this *is* the tourist season ..."

"Aren't we staying here?" Andy asked from the back seat.

"No, son," his dad answered, as he wheeled the van out of the packed hotel parking lot and toward the Interstate ramp. "We have to go on."

"But I'm tired," the boy whined, "and there's not enough light anymore to play my game!"

Annoyed—more with their current predicament

than with her son—Laura picked up a small white sack on the seat next to her and threw it to Andy, hitting him on the arm. "Here . . . have some fudge," she said flatly.

"I don't *like* fudge!" the boy retorted, and threw the sack back at his mom, smacking her on the head.

"Andy!" Pete said sharply, looking at his son in the rear-view mirror. "That's five points! When you get to ten, you lose your Turbo-Express for a week, remember?"

"Well, *she* started it!" he protested.

"Six," his father said.

The van fell silent, the air tense and heavy with more than the humidity of the on-coming storm. Big drops of rain splattered on the windshield. The sky was crying, and suddenly Laura felt like crying, too. She stared at the dark highway before her, upset that their wonderful day had turned sour.

"We shouldn't have stopped at the Dells," she sighed.

It had to be said, and it might as well be said by her, because she was the one who first suggested the detour to the expensive touristy playground . . .

A sign on the road advertising the Oak Street Antiques Mall had caught her attention, but Pete and Andy had just groaned.

Then Andy saw the gigantic 3-D billboard for Pirate's Cove—a 72-hole miniature golf course set in tiers of sandstone and waterfalls that overlooked the Wisconsin River. Quickly he defected to his mother's side.

Pete, reminding them both of their agreement to make it from Illinois to Minnesota, by nightfall—where a coveted condominium at Kavanaugh's Resort in Brainerd awaited them—held firm . . . until he drove over the next hill on the highway.

There, among the trees, was a pretty blonde braided billboard fraulein wearing an alluring peasant dress; she beckoned to him with her wooden finger, teasingly, tempting him to taste the homemade fudge (sixteen flavors) at the German Candy Shoppe.

"Well," Pete had said, slowly, "maybe we can stop for just a little while."

But "just a little while" turned into all afternoon, because there was much more to the Wisconsin Dells than antiquing and golfing and rich gooey fudge—like river rides and go-carts, wax museums and haunted houses . . .

"Let's try that one," Laura suggested, as a road-side motel materialized in the mist. Three hours earlier, she wouldn't have dreamed of ever stopping at such a scuzzy place; but now they were desperate, and *any* bed looked good, even this biker's haven.

Pete pulled off the highway and into the motel—a long, one-story, run-down succession of tiny rooms. The lot was full of pick-up trucks and motorcycles, so he parked in front of the entrance, and got out of the van, leaving the engine running.

Laura locked the doors behind him, and waited. Rain pelted the windshield. The van's huge wipers moved back and forth spastically, like gigantic grasshopper legs, grating on her nerves. She leaned over and shut the engine off.

Behind her, Andy sighed wearily.

Please, dear God, she thought, *let there be a room so we don't have to sleep in the car.* She strained to see through the rain-streaked window, trying to spot Pete. He'd been gone a long time, this time . . . too long.

That wasn't a good sign, either.

Suddenly Laura saw him dart in front of the van, and quickly she unlocked the doors. He jumped inside. His clothes were soaked, hair matted, but he wore a grin.

"You got us a room!" Laura cried, elated.

Pete nodded, wiping wetness from his face with the back of one hand. "But not here."

"Then where?"

He looked at her. "When I went in," he explained, "the desk clerk was telling another family they had no rooms . . . so, naturally, I turned around to leave. Then a maintenance man gave me a tip on a place ... a *bed and breakfast."*

"Oh, really?" They'd never stayed at one.

"I used the payphone and called," Pete continued. "The woman sounded very nice. They had one room left and promised to save it for us. I got the directions right here."

He fished around in his pocket and drew out a piece of paper.

"We gotta go back about forty miles, and it's a little out of our way, but ..."

"But it's a *bed,*" she smiled, relieved, throwing her arms around Pete, hugging him.

"And *breakfast,*" he smiled back, and kissed her.

"What's a bed and breakfast?" Andy asked.

Laura looked at her son. "A bed and breakfast is not really a hotel," she answered. "It's somebody's home." She paused. "It'll be like staying at your Aunt Millie's house."

"Oh," the boy said sullenly, "then I gotta be good."

"You've got to be *especially* good," Pete said, "because these people don't usually take children, but they're going to make an exception for us. Okay, son?"

"I'll try," he said, but not very convincingly.

An hour later, as the storm began to die down, the little family drove into the small quaint town of Tranquility, its old cobble-stone streets shiny from the rain.

At a big County Market grocery store, Pete turned left, down an avenue lined with sprawling oak trees and old homes set back from the street.

They pulled up in front of a many-gabled house. An outside light was on, illuminating the large porch, which wrapped around the front of the home. On either side of the steps sat twin lions, their mouths open in a fierce frozen roar as they guarded the front door.

Laura clasped her hands together, gazing at the house. "Oh, isn't it *charming?* This will be such fun!"

Pete nodded, then read the wooden sign attached to the sharp spears of the wrought iron gate. *"Die Gasthaus . . . ?"*

"That's German for 'the inn,' " Laura said, utilizing her high-school foreign language class for the very first time.

"So let's go in," smiled Pete.

"What's German for 'Splatterhouse'?" said a small sarcastic voice from the back seat.

Anger ignited in Laura—why did the boy have to ruin things? And after all they had done for him today! She turned to reprimand Andy, but her husband beat her to it.

"Shape up," Pete shouted at the boy. "You already have six points—wanna try for seven?"

"No."

"It's going to be a mighty long trip without your Turbo Express!" his father threatened.

"I'm sorry," Andy said. "It's not *my* fault this place looks like a spook house ..."

Pete wagged a finger at his son. "Now we're going to go in, and you're going to behave, and, goddamnit, we're all going to have a *good time!"*

There was a long silence.

Laura couldn't stand it, so she reached back and patted Andy on the knee. "Now gather up your things, honey," she said cheerfully. "Don't you know how lucky we are to be here?"

In the parlor of Die Gasthaus Bed and Breakfast, Marvin Butz sipped his tea from a china cup as he sat in a Queen Anne needlepoint chair in front of a crackling fireplace.

A bachelor, pushing fifty, slightly over-weight,

with thinning gray hair and a goatee, the regional sales manager of Midwest Wholesale Grocery Distributors was enjoying the solitude of the rainy evening.

Whenever he went on the road, Marvin always stayed at bed and breakfasts, avoiding the noisy, crowded, kid-infested chain hotels. The last thing he needed in his high-pressure job was being kept awake all night by a drunken wedding reception, or rowdy class reunion, or a loud bar band . . .

Besides, he delighted in being surrounded by the finer things in life—rare antiques, crisply starched linens, delicate bone china—which reminded him of his mother's home, before the family went bankrupt and had to sell everything.

He couldn't find these "finer things in life" in a regular hotel, where lamps and pictures and clock-radios were bolted down, like he might be some common thief. (Besides which, who would want such *bourgeois* kitsch, anyway?) And he could *never* get any satisfaction—or *compensation*—for the many inconveniences that always happened to him in the usual hotels. Whenever he complained, all he ever got was rude behavior from arrogant desk clerks.

But at most bed and breakfasts, even the smallest complaint, Marvin found, almost guaranteed a reduction in his bill. Why, half the time, he stayed for free! (Charging his expense account the full amount, of course.)

"More tea, Mr. Butz?"

Mrs. Hilger, who owned and ran the establishment

with her husband, stood next to Marvin, a Royal Hanover green teapot in her hand, a white linen napkin held under its spout to catch any drip. She was a large woman—not fat—just big. Marvin guessed her age to be about sixty, and at one time she must have been a looker, but now her skin was wrinkled, and spotted with old-age marks, her hair coarse and gray and pulled back in a bun.

He nodded and held out his cup. "With sugar."

"I'll bring you some."

He watched her walk away. She was nice enough, he thought, but the woman would talk his ear off if he let her. When he first arrived around six p.m., she started in lecturing him about how everybody should be nice to one another, and do what they could to make the world a better place to live—if he had known he was going to be staying with a *religious fanatic,* he never would have come there!

He frankly told her *his* world would be a better place to live if she would leave him alone while he unpacked!

She had acted hurt, and scurried off, and he hadn't seen her until about eight o'clock, when she had offered him tea.

Mrs. Hilger came back into the parlor, carrying a silver sugar bowl. She handed Marvin an unusual sterling sugar spoon with what appeared to be real rubies set into the handle.

He took the spoon and looked at it closely. "I've never seen anything like this before," he mused.

"That's because it's one of a kind," she replied.

He used the spoon to sugar his tea, then set it on the side of his saucer.

"There'll be another party coming in this evening," the woman informed him. "A couple with their young son."

About to take a sip of the tea, Marvin looked at her sharply. "But you advertised 'no children,' " he complained.

"Yes, I know," the woman said, "but this poor family is caught out in the storm without hotel accommodations."

"So *I'm* to be inconvenienced because some dumb hicks didn't have the common sense to make reservations?"

There was a brief silence. Then Mrs. Hilger said, "If that's how you feel, Mr. Butz, your stay with us will be complimentary."

Marvin smiled.

And Mrs. Hilger smiled back, but he wasn't at all sure that the smile was friendly.

Mr. Hilger's large form filled the doorway to the parlor. He looked more like a handyman than the proprietor of a bed and breakfast, in his plaid shirt and overalls.

Marvin had had a brief conversation with the bald, bespectacled man earlier, when Marvin had gone into the kitchen to admire an old butcher's block. Mr. Hilger had come up from the basement.

"It's from our store," Mr. Hilger had said. "We had

a little corner grocery before County Market came in and put us out of business."

"What a pity," Marvin had said, shrugging. "But, personally, I don't believe anybody gets 'put out of business' by anybody else."

"Oh?"

"Yes. You do it to yourself, by not keeping up. Survival of the fittest."

"You're probably right," Mr. Hilger had said, getting a butcher's apron out of a narrow closet by the pantry. The big man slipped it on and went back down into the basement.

Marvin had frowned—was food preparation going on down there? If so, he hoped conditions were sanitary.

"Those folks with the child are here," Mr. Hilger was saying to his wife. The apron was gone, now. "I'm going to help them with their luggage."

"Thank you, dear," Mrs. Hilger replied.

Marvin quickly finished the last of his tea and stood up. "I'll be retiring, now," he informed her. He'd rather die than spend one minute in boring, pointless small talk with these new people. "Please inform that family I will be using the bathroom at six in the morning. And I'd like my breakfast served promptly at seven, out in the garden."

"Yes, Mr. Butz," Mrs. Hilger nodded. "Good night."

Marvin left the parlor, through the main foyer and past a large, hand-carved grandfather clock. He climbed the grand oak staircase to the second floor.

To the left was the Gold Room, where an elderly couple from Iowa was staying. They had gone to bed already, the little woman not feeling well, and so their door was shut. But behind the door was a grandiose three-piece Victorian bedroom set of butternut and walnut, with a carved fruit cluster at the top of the headboard and dresser. (He had peeked in, earlier, when they were momentarily out.) He wished he had that room, because it had its own bath . . . but the old farts had gotten there first. At the end of the hall on the left was the White Room. The bridal suite. Everything in it was white—from the painted four-poster bed with lace canopy to the white marble-topped dresser. It also had its own bathroom. He'd gotten to see the exquisite room when he first arrived, and wouldn't have minded his company paying a little extra for such fine accommodations . . .

Some newlyweds on a cross-country honeymoon were in there right now—doing God only knows what behind their closed door.

Across the hall from the White Room, was the Blue Room, the least impressive (or so he thought). It was decorated in wicker, with a Battenburg lace comforter, and a collection of old cast-iron toys showcased on the ledges of the beveled glass windows. Mrs. Hilger had tried to put him in there, but he protested (the furnishings were so informal, it would have been like sleeping on a porch!). He demanded a different room.

The door to the Blue Room stood open, awaiting

the inconsiderate family that would soon be clomping nosily up the steps.

To the immediate right was the Red Room, his room, which had a massive oak bedroom set with eight-inch columns and carved capitals, and a beautiful red oriental rug on the floor. It was satisfactory.

Marvin used an old skeleton key to open his door; he had locked it, to protect his belongings, even though the other skeleton room keys could also open his door. He would have to speak to Mrs. Hilger, later, about this little breach in security.

He entered the room, leaving the door open. He was planning on getting his shaving kit and using the bathroom, which he shared with the Blue Room, before turning in for the night, but he stopped at a small mahogany table next to the door. On the table was a lovely cranberry lamp with a thumbprint shade and dropped crystals.

Marvin dug into his jacket pocket and pulled out the sweet little sugar spoon, and leaned over and turned on the lamp to examine the spoon better. Its red ruby handle sparkled in the light.

A nice addition to his spoon collection.

Suddenly, something caught his attention in the hallway. Flustered, caught off-guard, Marvin shoved the spoon back into his pocket and looked up from the light.

A young boy stood in the hall, not six feet away. How long the kid had been there, watching, Marvin didn't know.

Marvin reached out with one hand and slammed his door in the boy's face.

How he hated children! They were a bunch of sneaky, snooping, immature brats.

Marvin yawned, for the first time aware of how tired he was. He got his toiletries and went off to the bathroom, then came back and got into a pair of silk burgundy pajamas.

He crawled under the beige crocheted bedspread and lace-trimmed sheets. He wanted to read awhile, but his eyes were too heavy. He got out of bed, and turned off the pushbutton light switch on the wall by the door.

Then he went back to bed.

Soon, Marvin was fast asleep.

It was a deep sleep. So deep he didn't hear the skeleton key working in the keyhole of his door. Or see the dark form of Mr. Hilger poised over him, large hands out-stretched.

But not so deep that he didn't feel those hands tighten around his neck like a vise, slowly squeezing him into the deepest of all deep sleeps.

A noise woke Andy. It was a bump, or a thump, or *something*. He lay quietly in the dark on the cot Mrs. Hilger fixed up for him, and listened.

All was silent, now, except for the soft breathing of his parents across the room in that great big bed. Whatever the noise had been, Andy was glad it woke him. He'd been having a nightmare. A bad dream where he'd been sucked into the video game, *Splat-*

terhouse, he'd been playing. And ghouls and monsters were chasing him with butcher knives and stuff.

Andy reached under the cot and got his glasses and put them on. A fancy clock on a table read a quarter to three in the morning. He sat up further and looked at the window next to him. On the ledge was a row of small toys—little cars, and airplanes and trains. His mother told him they were antiques, and not to touch them.

Andy's favorite was the train. You could actually see the conductor standing inside! He picked the heavy toy up and held it in his hand. It was so much cooler than anything you ever saw in a toy store today! He reached under the cot again, opened his suitcase, and tucked the train inside. Then he lay back down.

There were so many of the toys—thirty-two, he'd counted—that he was sure the Hilgers wouldn't miss it. Besides, the boy thought, wasn't his mom always saying to his dad when they stayed in hotels, "Honey, take the soap, take the shampoo, get the Kleenex . . ."? This wasn't exactly soap, or shampoo, or Kleenex, but then this wasn't exactly a hotel. So it had to be kind of the same . . .

And if that nasty, mean man in the room next to them could cop a spoon, why couldn't he have the train? Andy *knew* the man had stolen it, because of the look on his face— there was guilt written all over it!

Andy had to pee. He remembered his mother telling him that if he woke up in the night to be sure and go, because someone else might be in the bathroom in the morning.

The boy got up from the cot and quietly slipped out of the room. He tiptoed down the dark hallway to the bathroom.

Inside, he used the toilet, which had a funny chain he had to pull to flush it. Then he washed his hands at a neat faucet where the water came out of a fish's head. He turned out the bathroom light, opened the door and stepped out in the hallway.

That's when he saw Mrs. Hilger coming out of the crabby man's room. She had some wadded-up sheets in her arms.

The woman didn't see him, because she had her back to the boy, heading toward the stairs with her bundle.

Andy stood frozen for a moment, and when the woman was gone, he walked down to that mean man's room.

The door was wide open. And even though the only light came from the moon that shone in through the windows, he could see that the bed had been made. There was no sign of that man *or* his things.

Andy tiptoed to the top of the stairs, which yawned down into blackness. Below, somewhere, he could hear noises—faint pounding and the sound of something electrical, something sawing, maybe, like his father sometimes used in the garage.

Quietly, he crept down the stairs, staying close to the railing, until he reached the bottom.

Suddenly, the big clock by the stairs bonged three times, scaring Andy nearly out of his skin! He waited until he'd calmed down then moved silently along, toward the back of the dark house, through the dining room with its big, long table. He bumped into a chair, and its legs went *Screech!* on the wooden floor.

Andy froze. The faint noises below him stopped. He held his breath. Seconds felt like minutes. Then the sounds started up again. He went into the kitchen.

There was a light coming from under the door that led to the basement. That's where the noises were coming from.

Andy thought about a movie he had seen last year with his father. At one point a kid—a boy just about like himself—was going to go down in a basement where bad, evil people lived. Andy had turned to his dad and said, "Why's he going down there?" And Andy's father had said, "Because it's a story, and he just has to *know.*"

And now, just like the boy in that scary movie, Andy reached his hand out for the doorknob. He didn't know why—he was certainly frightened—but he couldn't seem to stop himself!

Slowly, he opened the door to the basement, and the sound of sawing increased as the crack of bright light widened until Andy was washed in illumination. *What am I doing?* he thought, *I don't have to know!* And as he was starting to ease the door shut again, a hand settled on his shoulder.

He jumped. Someone was beside him! Shaking, he looked back at the shape of a figure with a knife in its hand, and gasped.

"What are you doing, young man?" the figure demanded.

The voice was low and cold—but a lady's voice.

Then there was a click and he saw her, one hand on the light switch, the other holding the butcher knife: Mrs. Hilger. The face that had been so friendly before was now very cross.

Even though Andy was trembling badly, he managed to say, "Wh-where am I? I ... I must be sleep-walking again."

There was a long, horrible moment.

Then the knife disappeared behind Mrs. Hilger's back and she said sweetly, "You're in the kitchen, my boy. I'll see that you get back to your room."

"Th-that's all right, now I know where I am."

He backed away from her and turned and hurried through the dining room, and when he got to the stairs, he bolted up them, and dashed down the hallway, past the man's room who had stolen the spoon, to his parent's room, where he opened the door, then slammed it shut, ran to their bed and jumped in between them.

"Andy!" his mother moaned. "What in the world ...?"

"Can I please sleep here, Mom?" he pleaded. "I had a terrible nightmare."

She sighed. "Well, all right, get under the covers."

Andy started to crawl beneath the sheets, but stopped.

"Wait," he said. "There's something I gotta do first."

He climbed out of the bed and went over to the cot, dug beneath it and got into his suitcase.

He put the toy train back on the ledge of the window.

Pete woke to a sunny morning, the smell of freshly brewed coffee and the unmistakable aroma of breakfast. He breathed deeply, taking in the wonderful smells.

He looked over at Laura, still sleeping soundly in the big bed next to him, her hair spread out on the lace pillowcase like a fan. She was so beautiful—even snoring, with her mouth open.

He propped himself up with both elbows and noticed his son sitting on the cot across the room, fully dressed, his little suitcase, packed, by his feet. The boy was staring at him.

"Hey, partner," Pete said, still a little groggy, "what's the hurry?"

Andy didn't respond.

Now Pete realized something was wrong with the boy, and vaguely remembered his son sleeping with them in the night.

Pete sat up further in the bed, letting the bedspread fall down around his waist. "Did you have a bad dream?" he asked.

The boy nodded. "Sort of."

"Well, why don't you come over here and tell me about it." Pete patted a place on the bed next to himself. "Most bad dreams sound pretty silly in the light of day."

Andy stood up slowly and went to the bed and sat on it. The springs made a little squeak.

Pete gazed at his son's face ... his large brown eyes, made larger by the glasses, his little pug nose, the tiny black mole on the side of his cheek . . . the depth of Pete's love for the child was sometimes frightening.

"You know that man in the room next to us?" Andy said almost in a whisper, looking at his hands in his lap.

"The one who had dibs on the bathroom from six to seven this morning?"

Andy nodded.

Pete waited.

"When I went to the bathroom in the middle of the night," Andy said, "he was *gone.*"

"Gone?"

Now the boy looked at his father. "His room was all made up, Dad . . . like he'd never been there!"

"Soooo," Pete said slowly, "what do you think happened?"

"I don't know," Andy said softly.

Pete looked toward the door of their room, and then back at his son. "Do you think somebody chopped him up with a meat cleaver," Pete said with a tiny smile, "and buried him in the garden, like in that movie we saw?"

Andy's eyes went wide, but then he smiled. *"No,"* he said. "I *guess* not." He paused. "But where *did* he go?"

Pete put an arm around the boy. "Son, Mrs. Hilger told me about that man ... He was very unhappy. And unhappy adults sometimes do unpredictable things. He just packed up and left."

"Really?"

"Sure." Pete hugged his son. "Now do you feel better?"

"Uh-huh."

"Okay." Pete slapped Andy's knee with one hand. "Let's wake up your mom and get down to breakfast, so we can get on the road!"

Breakfast at Die Gasthaus was offered in either the formal dining room, outside on the patio, or in the privacy of the rooms.

The elderly couple staying in the Gold Room had decided to eat in the dining room; the wife was feeling much better this morning after a good night's sleep.

The newlyweds, not surprisingly, were being served in their room.

Pete let Laura decide where they would eat—that was the kind of decision she always made, anyway—and she wanted to go out on the patio.

The three sat at a white wrought-iron table, with comfortable floral cushions on their chairs, surrounded by a variety of flowers.

Pete leaned toward Andy, and whispered that there didn't appear to be any new additions in the garden today.

Andy smiled. Laura asked what the two of them were talking about, and they both said, "Nothing."

Then Mrs. Hilger appeared in a starched white apron, carrying a casserole dish, which she placed in the center of the table. Pete leaned forward.

It was an egg dish, a souffle or something, and looked delicious—white and yellow cheeses baked over golden eggs with crispy bits of meat. Pete's mouth began to water.

"Oh, Mrs. Hilger," Laura said, "our stay here has been so wonderful!"

"I'm glad, dear," Mrs. Hilger replied, as she gave each of them a serving on a china plate. "My husband and I enjoy making other people happy . . . people who are appreciative, that is. And we try, in our small way, to do what we can to make this world a better place to live."

Pete, wolfing down the eggs, said, in between bites, "What's in this, Mrs. Hilger? Is it ham?"

"No," Mrs. Hilger said.

"Well, it's not sausage," Pete insisted.

Mrs. Hilger shook her head.

"Then, what is it?"

Mrs. Hilger smiled. "I'm sorry, but we never give out our recipes," she said. "Our unique dishes are one of the reasons people come back . . . most of them, that is."

Mrs. Hilger reached for the silver coffeepot on the table. "More coffee?" she asked Laura.

"Please," Laura said. "With sugar."

The woman reached into the pocket of her apron and pulled out a spoon—a silver one with red stones on the handle; she handed the spoon to Laura.

"Oh, how beautiful," Laura said, looking at the spoon.

"There's not another like it," Mrs. Hilger said.

Suddenly Andy began to gag and cough, and the boy leaned over his plate and spit out a mouthful of food.

"Andrew!" Laura cried, shocked.

"Son, what's the matter?" Pete asked, alarmed. The boy must have choked on his breakfast.

"I . . . I'm not hungry ..." Andy said, his face ashen as he pushed his plate away from himself.

"Andy!" Laura said, sternly. "You're being rude!"

But Pete stepped in to defend the boy. "He had kind of a rough night, Laura. That's probably why he doesn't have an appetite. Let's just forget it."

Laura smiled. "Well, I certainly have an appetite! Mrs. Hilger, I'd love some more of your delicious eggs . . . but I don't want to trouble you, I can get it myself." Laura started to reach for the dish, but Mrs. Hilger picked it up.

"Nonsense, my dear," the woman said with a tiny smile, and she put another huge spoonful of eggs with the cheeses and succulent meat on Laura's plate. "It's no trouble. We at Die Gasthaus just love to serve our guests!"

Cat's-eye Witness

Pierce Hartwell removed the pillow from his wife's face, relieved to see her expression was not one of agony, but peace. She had not suffered. She had, as Pierce expected her death certificate would verify, passed away in her sleep.

The lanky, darkly handsome, pencil-mustached Pierce, wearing the wine-color silk robe he'd received from Esther on their tenth anniversary not long ago, took one step back, pillow still held delicately in two hands as if he had brought it to his wife's bedside to present her with comfort, not oblivion. He stood poised there, as if waiting for Esther to wake up, knowing—hoping—she would not. The once beautiful, now withered features of the eighty-year-old woman had a calm cast, the simple white nightgown almost suggesting a hospital garment.

"Goodbye, darling," he whispered to the dead woman, feeling something almost like sadness. He was breathing hard, as hard as when of late he'd made love to the woman, an act that had increasingly taken his full effort and intense concentration.

When he had married Esther Balmfry ten years ago, she had been an attractive matron, slender and elegant on the cruise-ship dance floor. Pierce, at that time forty-five and wearying of his gigolo existence, had considered Esther a prime candidate for settling down. Prior to this, he had flitted from one fading flower to another, providing love in return for financial favors; but he had never married. Never considered it.

But—on that cruise ship a decade ago—Pierce had noticed several others of his ilk plucking the faded flowers from his field, men younger, newer at the game, fresher. Pierce had begun dyeing his hair, and wearing a stomach-flattening brace (he could never, even mentally, bring himself to say "girdle"), and had sensed that perhaps it was time to settle down. Pick one rich old girl who he could put up with for a few years before that "tragic" day when his beloved went where all rich old widows eventually go.

And Esther was childless, had no close relatives—except for Pierce, of course. Her loving husband.

These ten years with Esther had been increasingly difficult. The remnants of her beauty waned, though her health remained steadfastly sound. Her last physical—a few weeks ago—had elicited a virtual rave review from her doctor, who said she had the body of a woman twenty years younger.

That was easy for the doctor to say: the doctor hadn't had to sleep with her.

"My mother lived to see one hundred," Esther had announced over muffins and tea last week in the breakfast nook, her creped neck waving good morning to him. "And father lived to be ninety-eight."

"Really," Pierce had said, spreading strawberry jam on his muffin.

"Looks like you're going to be stuck with me for a while, darling," she'd said, patting his hand.

He'd always been given a generous allowance, but Pierce knew that Esther's fortune was a considerable one, and the life he could lead with access to that kind of cash would go a long way toward making up for the indignities of the last ten years. At fifty-five, he had living left to do. If he waited around for Esther to pass away of natural causes, he'd be a geezer, himself.

Or, if her health did finally go, but gradually, that fortune could be decimated by medical bills.

Pierce didn't dislike Esther, though he certainly didn't love her. He didn't feel much of anything for her, really: she was just a means to an end. And now her end could be his means to a new, unencumbered life.

And then there was that goddamned cat: that had been another factor, another catalyst to spark this unpleasant but necessary deed.

Clarence, the mangy brown beast, named for her late husband, had turned up at the door last year and Esther had welcomed it in, grooming it, taking it to the vet to be "fixed," lavishing attention upon the thing as if were a child. Pierce and the cat kept their distance—once the cat learned that Pierce would kick it or toss something its way, any time its mistress wasn't about—but just the presence of the animal meant distress to Pierce, who was after all allergic to cats.

His first act, as the master of the house, the sole human inhabitant of the near mansion (they had no live-in household staff), would be to toss that animal back out into the winter night, into the cold world from which it had emerged.

Just thinking about the beast—as Pierce stood at the bedside, taking his wife's pulse, making sure she was in fact deceased—made his eyes burn, his nose twitch.

No . . . that was no psychosomatic response: *that wretched animal was somewhere nearby!*

Pierce turned sharply and there it was: sitting like some Egyptian statue of a feline, the blue-eyed brown beast stared at him, eyes in unblinking accusation.

"Did you witness it, then?" Pierce said to the animal. "Did you see what I did to your mistress?"

It cocked its head at him.

Sniffling, Pierce said, "I liked *her . . .* Imagine what I'll do to you."

And he hurled the pillow at the creature.

But Clarence leapt nimbly from harm's way, onto the plush carpet, padding silently but quickly out of the bedroom, a blur of brown.

Pierce ran after the animal, chasing it down the curving stairs, past paintings by American masters, into a vast dark living room where the cat's tiny claws had damaged precious Duncan Phyfe antiques. The thing scampered behind a davenport and Pierce threw on the lights, pulled out the heavy piece of furniture . . . but the cat was gone.

For hours he stalked the house, with a rolled-up newspaper in hand, looking behind furniture, searching this nook and that cranny of the expansive, six-bedroom spread, checking in closets and in the basement and the most absurdly unlikely of places . . . even under the bed where his late wife slept her dreamless sleep.

No sign of Clarence.

By dawn Pierce had given up the chase, figuring the cat had found some way out of the house. Exhausted, he sat in the breakfast nook with a cup of coffee and drinking the bitter brew, wondering if it was too early to phone 911 about the unsettling discovery of his deceased wife next to him in bed. He raised the cup to his lips and the cat jumped up onto the table and stared at him with its deep blue unblinking accusatory eyes.

I saw what you did, the cat seemed to say.

Spilling his coffee, Pierce reached for its throat, but the beast deftly, mockingly, dove to the floor and scampered across the well-waxed tiles and into the living room.

Racing after it, Pierce spent another hour searching high and low, before he finally gave up—and realized the house was in a terrible disarray from his search. It took better than an hour to straighten the furniture, smooth various throw rugs and otherwise make the place look as normal as possible.

At eight o'clock Pierce called 911, working up considerable alarm as he said, "Come quickly! I can't rouse my wife! She won't wake up!"

The paramedics came, and Pierce—not even taking time to dress—accompanied them in the ambulance, but Esther was of course D.O.A. at the emergency room. Rigor mortis had begun to sink in. He put on his best distraught act, working up some tears, moaning to the attending physician about his inadequacy as a husband.

"If only I'd been awake!" Pierce said. "To think I was asleep beside her, even as she lay dying!"

This melodrama seemed to convince the doctor, who calmed Pierce, saying, "There's no need to blame yourself for this, Mr. Hartwell. There's every indication that your wife slipped away peacefully in her sleep."

"I ... I guess I'll have to find solace in that, won't I?"

By eleven a.m., Pierce was back home, driven there by one of the ambulance attendants. He was whistling as he went up the curving stairway, almost racing to the bedroom where he had murdered his wife. He went to the closet to select appropriately somber apparel for the day—there were arrangements to make, starting with the funeral home—and when he reached for his charcoal suit coat, the cat leapt from the shelf above, as if jumping right at him.

But it wasn't: Clarence scampered up onto the bed and resumed its Egyptian-style posture and again affixed its blankly reproachful blue-eyed gaze at him. Pierce moved slowly toward the animal, which twitched its nose; as if at this bidding, Pierce's own nose twitched, and began to run, his eyes starting to burn. He leapt at the cat with clawed hands, but the animal adroitly avoided its master's grasp and again fled the bedroom. This time Pierce did not follow. He sat on the edge of the bed, at its foot, and caught his breath. Slowly the symptoms of his allergy eased, and he rose and finished dressing.

The cat's next appearance came when Pierce was seated in his study, at the desk, calling the Ferndale Funeral Home. He was halfway through the conversation with the undertaker when the cat nimbly jumped up onto the desk, just out of his reach, and stared at him as he completed his phone conversation. Gradually the allergy symptoms returned, his eyes watering, burning, puffing up.

The undertaker, hearing Pierce's sniffling, said, "I know this must be a difficult time for you, Mr. Hartwell."

"Thank you, Mr. Ballard. It has been difficult."

And as Pierce hung up the phone, the cat sprang from the desk and scurried out of the room.

Pierce didn't bother following it.

The police came that afternoon, two of them, plainclothes detectives, a craggy thickset lieutenant named March with eyebrows as wild as cat's whiskers, and a

younger detective named Anderson, ruggedly handsome but also quietly sullen.

Pierce knew Lt. March, a bit, as the onetime Chicago homicide cop had married a wealthy widow
several years before, the couple a staple of country
club dances, where the detective was viewed as a
"character" among the city's captains of industry and
inheritors of wealth.

They sat in the study, with Pierce behind the desk,
the two men across from him, as if this were a business appointment. Pierce hadn't offered to take their
topcoats and neither men took them off, as they sat
and talked—a good sign. This wouldn't take long.

"Pierce," Lt. March said, with a familiarity that
wasn't quite earned, and with a thickness of speech
that reflected a stroke the detective had suffered a
year before, "I hope you know that you have our
deepest sympathy."

By "our," Pierce wasn't sure whether March was
referring to Mrs. March or his fellow detective, the
younger man whose unblinking gaze seemed to contain at least a hint of suspicion.

"I appreciate that . . . Bill."

March smiled; one side of his face seemed
mildly affected from that stroke, and his speech
had a measured manner, as if every single word
had to be cooked in his mind before he served it
up. "There is the formality of a statement. We can
do that here, if you'd like. Save you a trip to the
Public Safety Building."

"Certainly."

Anderson withdrew a small tape recorder from his topcoat pocket, clicked it on and set it, upright, on the edge of the desk. The recorder emitted a faint whirring.

"When did you discover that Esther had passed away?" March asked.

"When I woke up," Pierce said, and his nose began to twitch.

"What time was that, would you say?"

"Well, just minutes, probably moments, before I called 911. I didn't look at the clock." His eyes were running now; that cat—that cat was somewhere in this room! "Don't you record those calls?"

"Yes."

"So you can verify the time, that way."

"Yes we can."

Pierce felt a rustling at his feet; glancing down, he saw the damned thing, sitting under the desk, at his feet, staring up at him with those spooky unblinking blue eyes.

Sniffling, he reached for a tissue from a box on the desktop. Blew his nose, dried his eyes, and said, "Sorry, gentlemen."

"We know this is difficult for you," March said.

"Terribly difficult," Pierce said, and withdrew another tissue.

The statement was brief—what was there to tell?—but once the tape recorder had been clicked off, Anderson said, "We'd like you to authorize an autopsy, Mr. Hartwell."

"Why is that necessary?"

"I think you know."

There was something nasty about Anderson's tone, and Pierce said, huffily, "What are you implying, sir?"

March frowned at his partner, then, smiling at Pierce, sat forward. "Pierce, I'd like to be candid, if I might."

"Certainly."

"When a wealthy elderly woman—who has recently married a relatively younger man—dies under circumstances that are even remotely questionable, it's incumbent upon the police to investigate."

What did he mean, "relatively younger?"

"An autopsy," March continued, "should establish your wife's death by natural causes, and we can all go on with our lives."

"Bill," Pierce said, invoking the lieutenant's first name, "considering the fact that many people in our fair community have accused *you* of marrying for money, you're hardly anyone to—"

"Mrs. March isn't dead," Anderson interrupted.

"Gentlemen," March said, holding out two palms. "Please. This is an unfortunate situation ... a tragic situation. Let's not get into name-calling or personalities."

Eyes burning, Pierce said, "Of course I'll authorize an autopsy, distasteful though a debasement of my dear late wife's remains are to me. Just tell me what you need me to do."

When Pierce had seen the detectives out, he returned to his study, hoping the cat would still be in the well of the desk. Pierce's intention was to trap the cat, perhaps cage it up in a wastebasket and hurl the creature into the cold late afternoon air, where it could either fend for itself or freeze itself to death—preferably the latter.

But there was no sign of the cat. He looked everywhere, irritated but relatively calm, not allowing himself the indignity of turning the house topsy-turvy again, which would only require him to set it aright. Clearly the cat had finally sensed the obvious: that Pierce meant Clarence harm.

Sooner or later it would come out, to its water and food dishes.

So Pierce set out fresh water and food for the animal—the cat food liberally laced with rat poison—and, whistling, dressed for dinner.

Since they had no cook (Esther had enjoyed preparing breakfasts and lunches herself), the couple's habit was to dine out. In a town the size of Ferndale, only a handful of suitable restaurants presented themselves—the country club and the hotel, chiefly. Pierce chose the latter, not wanting to chance running into March and his wife at the former.

He was famished and hoped the staff at the hotel restaurant—who went out of their way to express their sympathy, to stop by and comment about how much they would miss the sweet, kind Esther—did not consider him callous, to eat so heavily and drink so heartily. He hoped they would consider him to be drowning his sorrows, as opposed to what he was really doing, which was celebrating.

At home, mildly tipsy and extremely drowsy, his stomach warm and full, Pierce lumbered up the curving stairs. When he found himself in the bedroom—the bedroom he and Esther had shared—a chill passed through the room, and him. Winter wind rattled frost-decorated windows. Telling himself he wanted to get away from the draft, he stumbled down the hall into one of the guest bedrooms.

Clothed in the Armani suit he'd worn to dinner, taking time only to step out of his Italian loafers, he flopped onto the bed, on his back. Had his conscience sent him into this bedroom? Did he feel guilty about what he'd done to Esther? These thoughts were worthy only of his laughter, with which he filled the room, laughing until his tiredness took over and sent him almost immediately into a deep sleep.

He awoke, not with a start, but gradually, groggily, with the growing sensation of pressure on his chest. He reached for the nightstand lamp, clicked it on, and stared into the blue unblinking eyes of the brown animal sitting on top of him.

Staring at him.

Staring into him.

The accusatory stare of the witness to the murder he'd committed. . . .

Screaming, Pierce sat up, flinging the cat off him. The beast rolled and came up running, scurrying out, claws clicking on the varnished wood of the hallway.

And Pierce was after the animal, chasing it down the winding stairs, darkness relieved only by moonlight filtering in through frosted windows. This time there would be no frantic search of the house. This time he would prevail.

As the cat headed into the living room, Pierce dove, and in a careening tackle that took over an end table and sent a lamp clattering, crashing, to the floor, Pierce scooped the animal in his arms and held it tight. Clarence fought, but its claws were facing outward as Pierce hugged it around the belly.

The nearest door was the front one, and, lugging the squirming beast, Pierce made his way there, holding tight around the cat's belly with one arm and with the other reaching to open the door, swinging it open, flinging the beast into the deadly cold night.

Slamming the door behind it.

No sounds came from beyond the closed door: that cat didn't want back inside, no matter how cold it was. For the longest time, Pierce sat on the floor with his back to the door, folding his arms tight, laughing, laughing, laughing, until tears were rolling down his cheeks, never aware exactly when the glee gave way to weeping.

At some point he found his way back to the bedroom, where, exhausted, he quickly fell to sleep. He had nightmares but on waking didn't remember them—they just clung to his mind the way the taste of sleep coated his mouth. But he was able to brush his teeth and deal with the latter; the taste of the un-remembered dreams stuck with him.

Nonetheless, the morning passed uneventfully, without any particular stress. Noting that the poi-soned cat food had not been touched, he emptied the bowl into the sink and down the garbage disposal. He washed his hands thoroughly before preparing himself an English muffin and coffee. He showered, shaved, and was feeling fairly refreshed, wearing the same silk robe he'd killed his wife in, when the phone rang.

"Could you come down here, to the Public Safety Building?" Lt. March asked.

"Am I needed?"

"We have the results of your wife's autopsy, and we'd like to discuss them with you . . . if it's not inconvenient."

At one o'clock, wearing a Pierre Cardin sports jacket and no tie, Pierce Hartwell walked to March's office on the first floor of the modern Ferndale Public Safety Building. The door to the modest office was open and March was seated behind his desk, with Anderson in a chair by a cement block wall.

And on top of the desk, seated off to the left like an oversize paperweight, was the cat.

Clarence.

Sitting and staring with its terrible blue eyes—right at Pierce.

"Have a seat," March said.

Swallowing, Pierce pulled a chair up, opposite March and as far away as possible from the brown beast. The goddamn thing looked none the worse for wear: no sign that it had spent a terrible frostbitten night, perfectly groomed, even purring, as it stared accusingly at Pierce.

March said, "Mr. Hartwell, there is a disturbing aspect that's turned up, in the autopsy."

"What . . . what are you talking about?"

The cat seemed to stare right through him. The cat. The witness. Could they somehow know this cat had witnessed the murder? The goddamn thing couldn't have told them. He was a cat!

March was saying, "Your wife's eyes ..."

The cat's eyes . . .

"... had severe hemorrhaging."

Pierce began sniffling. "Uh . . . uh, what do you mean?"

Anderson, sitting back, arms folded, said, "Clotting. The whites of your wife's eyes were so clotted with burst vessels they were damn near completely red."

From the nearby desktop, Clarence, the cat, stared at Pierce, whose eyes had begun to burn. *I saw what you did,* he seemed to say.

"A person suffering suffocation tries so hard to breathe," March said, "the blood vessels burst, in the eyes."

Eyes.

Cat's eyes . . .

His own eyes, burning, burning . . .

"We've been doing a background search on you, Mr. Hartwell," Anderson said. "You met your wife on a cruise ship, isn't that correct?"

"How could you know?" Pierce blurted.

"Very simple," Anderson said.

Pierce lurched forward in his chair. "You found it outside in the cold, didn't you? What did you do, go into my house and find that poisoned food? Did you have a warrant? Perhaps I should call my attorney."

The two detectives glanced at each other; but the cat was looking right at Pierce—and the animal seemed to shake its head, no. . . .

"He couldn't have told you anything," Pierce said, and laughed as he nodded toward Clarence. "A goddamn cat can't talk."

Anderson started to say something, but March waved a hand and the younger detective fell mute.

"Go on, Mr. Hartwell," March said.

"You're very clever, lieutenant. How did you do it? How could you know that that cat witnessed what I did?"

"*What* did you do, Mr. Hartwell?"

"You know damn good and well." Water was running from his eyes—not tears, just that burning goddamn allergy kicking in. "You just said so yourself. I smothered her—with a pillow. But she didn't suffer. I would never have done that. Never."

Nodding slowly, March got on the phone and called for a uniformed cop. Pierce just sat there, avoiding the gaze of the purring cat on the detective's desk. The damn thing seemed to be smiling, a Cheshire cat, now.

"If you'll go with this gentleman," March said, standing, gesturing past the animal to the police officer who was now standing in the doorway, "he'll escort you to a room where you can make your full statement. We'll be with you momentarily."

Pierce could only nod. He needed help to get to his feet and the police officer gave it to him.

"How did you know?" Pierce asked from the doorway, eyes watering, nose running. "How in God's name could you know about the cat?"

The two detectives said nothing.

Then Pierce was gone, and Anderson said, "That's one for the books. We could never have made our case on those clotted eyes alone. His gigolo background woulda helped, but . . ."

"Maybe he had a conscience."

"That guy?" Anderson snorted and waved at the air. "No way in hell."

Shrugging, March got on the phone and arranged for a technician to meet them at the interrogation room.

Then, hanging up, March shook his head and asked Anderson, "What do you suppose he was going on about?"

"What do you mean?"

"You know—that business about a cat?"

The two men widened their eyes, shrugged at each other and left the empty office, to take the confession.

Reunion Queen

Her mood darker than the night—and the night was very dark—the striking blonde tooled the candy-apple Jaguar into the Marriot lot. She climbed out, pausing by the car, standing there like a modern-day gunfighter, red-nailed fingers slowly opening and closing.

With a smile bordering on a smirk, she walked toward the hotel, ground fog swirling up around her legs, red stiletto heels clicking on the asphalt, punctuating the thunder growling in the distance.

At the entrance of the modern, sterile building, she stopped and looked up.

Above the double glass doors hung a homemade banner— WELCOME CLASS OF 1978—their fifteenth reunion; it flapped crazily in the breeze, as if trying to escape the imminent storm.

Her smile vanished, blue eyes clouded, as she gazed

at the sign; the wind whipped long blonde strands of hair around her face.

Lightning split the sky, and the world went white, then black. Big drops of rain began to pelt her, and the banner, its painted letters starting to bleed and run.

Her smile returned, and grew broader until she threw back her head, laughing, her throaty voice mingling with the thunder that followed.

She reached up and ripped the banner down, letting the wind take it.

Then she straightened her red lace dress, and adjusted each copious breast in the push-up bra, opened the glass doors and walked inside.

Heather sat at a table with Linda just outside the hotel ballroom on the second floor. They were collecting money for the banquet tickets and handing out I.D. badges, which displayed each classmate's name above their old high school yearbook photo.

Heather leaned toward Linda, touching the other woman's arm intimately as if the two of them were best of friends, and giggled as if she were having a great time . . . but inside Heather was seething.

How did I get stuck on the goddamn door? she fumed. *I'm the fucking class President!*

Heather smiled sweetly at Linda, who was reciting recent bowling scores, like it was somehow important. She studied her classmate's face and concluded that no amount of plastic surgery could help. If *she* were Linda, she'd kill herself.

"Would you like to go bowling sometime?" Linda

asked, under the deranged impression that spending the past hour with Heather made her a close friend— or a friend at all, for that matter.

"That sounds very entertaining," Heather answered. As in slicing and dicing a finger in the Cuisinart.

At the end of the carpeted corridor, three men burst out of the men's bathroom, laughing loudly, punching each other's arms. What was it about class reunions that regressed even a thirty-something hunk like her husband into a nerdy teenager?

"Rick!" Heather called out disgustedly.

He ignored her.

So she hollered louder. "Rick! Come here!"

Her husband, tall, handsome, so perfect in his Armani suit, shrugged at his other two friends—a fat farmer and balding banker—and sauntered toward her.

Heather felt her face flush; how *dare* he be having a good time when she was so miserable!

"Where's Jennifer?" she snapped at him. "She was supposed to take my place fifteen minutes ago!"

He looked at her stupidly. "Haven't seen her, hon."

"Well, *find* her, damnit! I'm sick of sitting here!"

Out of the corner of her eye, Heather could see Linda shifting uncomfortably in her chair; Heather didn't want to alienate the woman—not just yet—she might need her vote.

Heather gave Linda a patronizing, little smile. "It's just that, as *president,* I have other things to attend to," she explained.

Linda nodded and looked away.

Heather turned back to Rick. "Go . . . find . . . Jennifer, *dear.*"

"Okay, okay," he said, gesturing in a calm-down manner with both hands, "I'll go find her."

He winked at Linda.

Linda beamed.

"So *go,*" Heather said through clenched teeth. "And back off on the booze!"

"Yes, hon," he said and turned away.

Heather watched him move slowly down the hall, in no great hurry to accommodate her, which infuriated her further. Finally, Rick opened the ballroom doors, letting escape the loud, pounding disco music from their high school days, where it bounced off the walls in perfect timing with the beating of Heather's palpitating heart. . . . *staying' alive . . .*

The ballroom doors slammed shut; the corridor fell into a strained silence.

Linda cleared her throat and asked, "I wonder who's going to be crowned Reunion Queen?"

Heather, pretending not to care, began to straighten the remaining badges on the table. "Whoever gets the most votes," she said, but thought, *It damn well better be me.*

After all, wasn't *she,* even after fifteen years, still the best-looking woman in her class? And Heather had gone to great lengths and expense to make sure that she was: trips to the tanning salon, weight reduction classes, professional makeup and hair care (her shoulder-length brunette tresses completely untouched by gray—*now)*—not to mention a six-month-long search for the perfect little designer dress . . .

And for *what?* Heather thought sullenly, so she could rot out here, while everyone else was in the ballroom having fun?

Heather looked resentfully at Linda, whose mouth now hung open like a big bass being reeled in. What was the *matter* with her, anyway?

Heather followed Linda's stare to a woman who was ascending the stairs in front of them.

And Heather gasped—not because of the woman's hair, which was butter-blonde brushing bare shoulders, or her porcelain face, its features almost too perfect, or her voluptuous figure, which bordered on Amazonian—but because the *bitch* was wearing Heather's designer dress!

Perfectly balanced on her high heels, the blonde undulated toward them.

"Hi!" She said.

Linda continued to stare at the woman, but Heather said pleasantly, "The Bimbo Convention must be at some *other* hotel." After all, this was no one Heather knew from school.

"Pardon me?" The blonde looked confused, which Heather considered redundant.

"This is a *class reunion,*" Heather said, her voice dripping with insolence. "But then, I guess you couldn't read the sign outside."

The blonde flashed a dazzling white smile. "I'm afraid there is no sign . . . but I'm at the right place."

And she extended one hand, moving it over the remaining I.D. badges spread out on the table, like a fortune teller picking a tarot card, and with a perfectly manicured fingernail, tapped one. "That's me!" she said.

Linda leaned forward in her chair. "Hilda?" she asked, stunned. "Hilda Payne?"

"Hello, Linda," the blonde said warmly.

With a squeal, Linda jumped up, ran around the table and gave the blonde a hug.

"I can't believe it's you!" Linda said.

The blonde smiled. "It's been a long time. I'm sorry I couldn't make it back for the tenth."

"You . . . you look *wonderful,* '"Linda gushed.

"So do you," the blonde replied.

Gag me with a spoon, Heather thought. She studied the blonde, trying to mentally transform the homely girl on the badge into the gorgeous woman (all right, she admitted it) in front of her. But then, Heather really didn't remember Hilda much at all—or any of the other plain non-entities that had roamed the school hallways like cows, getting in her way.

"Are any of the other girls here?" the blonde asked Linda. "Mary? Diane?"

Linda nodded, her head jerking back and forth on her shoulders like a jack-in-the-box on a spring. "I can't *wait* until they see you!" she said excitedly.

And Linda began pulling the blonde by the arm down the hall toward the ballroom.

Heather stood up. "Hey, wait just a minute, Linda!"

she said angrily. "Who's gonna look after the *table?*"

"How about you?" Linda shot back.

And the two women disappeared through the ball-room doors.

. . . heart of glass . . .

Heather slammed her fists on the table, rattling the cash box and scattering the badges.

Then, dejectedly, she slumped in her chair.

"But she's wearing my dress," Heather whimpered to no one. "She wearing *my dress . . .*"

Rick leaned on the bar, a scotch and soda in hand, and surveyed the ballroom.

A few people had already taken seats at tables decorated in the school's colors—purple and gold—while others continued to mill around, trying to talk over the deafening disco music.

He hated those faggy songs. And he was embarrassed that his class had picked one of them as *their* song: "Disco Duck," for Christ's sake! Why couldn't he have been born earlier? Like his older brother, Ray, who was a senior in high school when the Beatles and Stones hit.

. . . she works hard for the money . . .

He took a drink, and shook his head. *She* should try working for a car dealership, he thought bitterly. Not that the work itself was hard. The hard part was having his wife's father own the business, and always being under the old man's thumb. Rick resented the hell out of him and Heather, who talked him into turning down that pro ball draft offer to go into the family business.

Maybe that was why Rick was always looking for love in all the wrong places . . .

His eyes locked with Jennifer's. The pretty, slender redhead was standing alone by the dance floor. He looked quickly away.

But then she was next to him, touching his arm lightly, wearing that hurt expression he detested.

"Look, Jen," he said carefully, not wanting his voice to carry too far, "sorry about last week ..."

"Can I see you tonight?" Her big brown eyes looked wet.

He avoided them, staring out across the room. "Maybe tomorrow," he said, and slowly moved away from her.

He *could have* seen Jennifer, if he'd wanted, but he didn't, because across the room, he'd seen somebody else . . .

She was standing by the ballroom doors, an incredible creature. But surrounding her were some of the skankiest broads in the entire class; they were fawning over her, attending to her, like she was the queen bee and they were the drones.

Suddenly the gorgeous babe flashed him a smile.

Yeah! He chugged his drink, and set it on a table as he moved toward her like a magnet to metal.

. . . *daya think I'm sexy* . . .

"Well, *hello,*" Rick said. "Come here often?"

She looked at him with sultry eyes. "Would you believe me if I said it was my very first time?"

He smirked. "No." He couldn't keep his eyes off her boobs; they looked like the real thing, not hard, fake implants like his wife's.

"I hope you're just trying to read my name tag," the blonde teased.

"Uh . . . yeah," he smiled, focusing on the badge's high school yearbook photo. God, what a dog she'd been!

"You don't remember me, do you?"

He shook his head. Not if she'd looked like that.

"Well," she smiled, "we didn't exactly have the same friends."

Flanking her, the drones glared at him. She could say that again.

"Come *on,* Hilda," one of them said. "Let's go find a table—by *ourselves.*"

"Perhaps I'll see you later," Rick said, reaching out, running his fingers sensuously down her arm.

"I'm almost sure of it," she smiled sexily. "Until then ..."

She held out one hand for him to shake. As he took it, he felt something hard in his palm.

He watched her as she wandered off with her friends.

Then he looked down at the hotel key-card in his hand. The number 310 was written on it.

. . . *macho macho man.* . .

He grinned.

In the ladies' lounge, Jennifer reached for a tissue on the marble vanity and blew her nose. The bathroom was empty; everyone else was enjoying the prime rib dinner. She wasn't hungry.

She looked at herself in the mirror and hated what she saw: a desperate middle-aged woman helplessly in love with a married man.

With a sob, she turned away from herself. She felt like a drug addict—only the drug she was addicted to wasn't crack or cocaine, it was Rick. And even though her mind warned, "Just say no," her heart refused to listen . . .

She had been in love with him since high school, but he'd been a jock and she a bookworm, and he never noticed her. But at the ten year reunion, that all changed; he swept her off her feet—and onto her back—after she'd dumped her date, and he'd ditched his wife. And Jennifer had been hooked ever since.

Now five years later, her life was a mess. She didn't date. She had no friends—they had long ago tired of hearing her woes—and energy that should have gone into advancing her career went instead into the stagnant affair. If she *only* had the strength to give him up! Yet, the thought of not seeing Rick—however sporadic and brief— threw her into a panic . . .

The lounge door opened and that blonde, Hilda, entered—the one she had seen Rick flirting with earlier. Jennifer couldn't believe Hilda would even speak to Rick after what he'd done to her so many years ago . . .

Hilda saw Jennifer and a small friendly smile formed.

"Well, hi, Jen," she said.

"Hilda," Jennifer replied coolly, pretending to fix her hair in the mirror. How she envied this woman, who seemed so happy and in control of her life.

Hilda walked over to the vanity and with a sigh of relief, kicked off her high heels. Then she dumped the contents of her gold purse on to the counter, picked out the lipstick, and applied the blood-red color to her lips.

"Don't tell me you're still carrying the torch for that *creep,*" Hilda said.

Jennifer turned away from the mirror; she didn't feel like discussing her situation with *anyone,* let alone some classmate she barely knew from high school.

She started to leave, but Hilda stepped back into her way.

"I know it's none of my business," Hilda said, her voice soft and reasoning, "but he's never going to leave Heather and marry you. Why should he? He's having his cake and eating it, too. You've got to face it."

Jennifer felt her face grow hot. "You're right, you know," she said. "You're absolutely right."

Hilda nodded smugly.

"It *is* none of your business!"

And she pushed past her.

"I'm glad my cousin Lenny isn't here to see you now," Hilda said behind her, almost contemptuously. "He thought you were the only smart, decent person in high school. I guess he was wrong."

Jennifer, her back to Hilda, hand on the door, hesitated. "I guess he was ..." she said softly.

But instead of leaving, Jennifer looked over her shoulder. "I didn't know Lenny was your cousin."

"Not many people did, even though we were in the same grade together. We didn't have the same last name."

Jennifer walked back toward Hilda. She thought there was a faint resemblance. "Tell me, how is Lenny?"

"Dead."

The way Hilda said it, so casually, so flippantly, made Jennifer feel like she'd been slapped; if she hadn't been immediately filled with sadness and memories of Lenny, she would have verbally lashed out at the woman.

But instead, Jennifer said, "I'm sorry . . . and I'm sorry he didn't have a better life; he was even more lost and miserable than I was in high school. But he was a good friend." Then she asked, "How . . . how did he die?"

"He killed himself."

Jennifer looked down at the floor, then back at Hilda. "I guess I'm not surprised," she said slowly. "But now I'll always wonder ... if he and I had stayed in touch . . . friends listen to friends, you know ..."

"They should."

Jennifer waited while Hilda gathered up the contents of her purse on the counter, and put on her shoes.

They left the lounge and walked back down the corridor toward the ballroom.

As they passed the vacant table in the hallway, Jennifer said archly, "I heard Heather went home to change her dress."

Hilda smiled. "It wasn't too hard to find out what she'd be wearing tonight," she replied, opening the ballroom door. "After all, she'd told everybody in town." . . . *bad girls* . . .

Bathed in the moonlight, Hilda stood nude by the open window in a room on the third floor of the hotel. One floor below, she could see her classmates, through the domed glass ceiling of the ballroom, still eating.

Muted music floated up to her.

. . . *more than a woman* . . .

There was a knock at the door.

She moved to the bed and slipped under the soft white sheets.

"Come in!" she called.

The door opened, then closed, and Rick stood at the foot of the bed.

"We don't have much time," he whispered conspiratorially, unbuttoning his shirt. "My wife will be looking for me."

Hilda stuck out her lower lip, pretending to pout. "Too bad," she said. "I guess I'll just have to settle for what I can get."

Quickly, Rick removed the rest of his clothing; they lay in a heap on the floor.

"Come and get it, big boy . . ." Hilda purred, patting a place next to herself on the bed.

. . . you're the one that I want. . .

Grinning like a kid Christmas morning, Rick climbed under the sheets, and pulled her roughly to him.

"What a bitchin' babe!" he said, his breath an unpleasant cocktail of cigarettes and booze.

He kissed her.

What a lousy lover, she thought.

He pulled back and peered in her face. "Look," he said, "I do remember you, now. And I hope you're not mad about that little joke . . . back in high school."

"Little joke?"

"You know ... me pretending to invite you to the senior prom, and all."

"And all?"

She sat up in the bed, letting the sheet slide down to expose her firm, round breasts. She leaned toward him.

"Now *why* should I be mad?" she said, running one long red fingernail down his cheek. "It was just a harmless prank . . . and I think a person should be able to handle a harmless prank, don't you?"

He started to say something, but there was a loud pounding at the door.

"Hilda!" a male voice hollered. "Are you in there? Open the door!"

"Oh, my God!" she whispered frantically. "It's my husband!"

Rick jumped out of the bed. "You didn't tell me you were married!" he whispered back, seeming more annoyed than frightened.

She shrugged. "You didn't ask... besides, you're married."

Quickly she got out of the bed, snatched a red silk robe off a nearby chair, and put it on. "You've got to hide!" she said. "The last man Butch caught me with landed up in the hospital for six months!"

"Butch?" he said. "Oh, great! Wonderful! And just *where* am I supposed to hide in this dinky room?"

She came around the bed and grabbed him by the arm. "Quick!" she said. "Under the bed."

Rick dropped to the floor and tried to squeeze beneath the boxsprings but he was too big.

She shook her head. "Nope. Too narrow."

He stood up again.

"Here," she said, pulling him over to a wardrobe which stood against the wall, "get inside."

She opened the cabinet and pushed him in among the clothes and hangers, but the door wouldn't close.

"Nope," she said, pulling him back out. "Too small."

"Why don't I just stand in the corner with a lampshade on my head?" he suggested sarcastically.

"Too obvious."

She looked toward the window.

"I know . . . climb out the window. You can stand on the ledge."

"Are you *nuts?* I'm not going out there!"

"Hilda!" the man bellowed from behind the door. "If there's somebody in there with you I'll kill the son-of-a-bitch!"

Rick climbed out the window. Cursing, he inched his way along the ledge.

Hilda scooped up his clothes and threw them out after him; they sailed down, landing on the dome of the ballroom, attracting the attention of a few people who looked up, which was just what she wanted.

"What the hell did you do that for?" Rick asked, exasperated, clinging to the wall.

"I can't have my husband finding your clothes! Now, don't worry, I'll get rid of him. Just stay put!"

"Like, where *else* would I go?"

. . . gonna fly now . . .

Hilda went to the door and opened it.

"Darling!" she said loudly. "I didn't mean to keep you waiting ... I was in the bathtub."

A burly man in a Marriot maintenance uniform smiled and held out his hand.

She reached into the pocket of her silk robe and handed him a hundred-dollar bill.

Outside the window came a terrific crash, following shouts and screams.

Hilda ran to the window and looked down.

Below, on the ballroom floor sprawled Rick; he looked like a baby bird in a nest of glass.

"Sweet Jesus!" said the maintenance man, now standing next to her. "You didn't say anything about anybody gettin' killed ..."

"How was I supposed to know he was going to fall?" she said, stunned. "I just wanted him *exposed.*"

"He's exposed, all right," the maintenance man

said, looking down. He pointed a thick thumb at himself. "I'm outta here, lady," he said. "I don't know you, and you don't know me."

And he left.

She stepped back from the window, into the shadows of the room. "It was just a harmless prank ..."

Heather returned to the ballroom just in time to join the group of her classmates who were gazing up through the glass dome, giggling at something. She joined in the laughter, at the sight of the naked man doing an ungainly tightrope act on the ledge of the floor above. Her laughter caught in her throat, however, as she recognized Rick, and then the group's glee turned to gasps as Rick fell, and they jumped back, as he crashed through in a shower of glass fragments.

She rushed to him.

Even before she knew if he was dead or alive, she bent near him where he lay, sprawled in a pile on his clothes and shards of glass. Those around saw only concern on her face, but her whispered words to her husband were: "This is the last time you humiliate me ... I want a divorce!"

He could only manage a moan.

Later, she turned her back on him, as ambulance attendants arrived to tend to her husband's cuts, and walked regally away.

She was a queen about to be crowned, after all, with a court to attend . . .

Hilda stood with her friends in the ballroom and watched as ambulance attendants carefully transferred

Rick on to a gurney. Now that it was apparent Rick's injures weren't life-threatening—falling on top of his clothes had kept him from being shredded—many of the spectators were snickering and laughing.

Jennifer walked up to Hilda. "You did that on purpose," she said acidly. "You set him up!"

"He set himself up," Hilda responded flatly.

There was a pause, then Jennifer blurted, "You're just full of surprises, aren't you?"

"Stick around . . ."

A screech filled the room—feedback from the P.A. system—as one of the reunion committee members, a tall, lanky sandy-haired man, spoke into the mike at the edge of the dance floor. "Everyone . . . please go back to your tables. In spite of this . . . unfortunate accident . . . the hotel will allow us to continue with our evening."

People began to return to their chairs. Several of the waiters were clearing away the last of the glass.

"I have the results of the ballots filled out during dinner," the committee member continued, holding up an envelope, "and the woman named Reunion Queen this evening will preside over tomorrow's pig roast."

A hush fell over the room.

He opened the envelope. "And the Reunion Queen is . . . Hilda Payne!"

Instantaneous squeals came from several tables, followed by loud applause.

Near the front, in a prominent position she'd taken, Heather stood amid her classmates, shocked; then she joined in, clapping, too loudly, her face frozen in a smile not even she believed.

Hilda walked slowly up to the microphone. She smiled and nodded at Heather, whose glazed smile seemed about to crack. Another classmate handed her a bouquet of red roses, and placed a small rhinestone tiara on her head.

She looked out over the audience: a sea of smiling faces.

"Thank you," she said, as the applause waned. "I think it's fitting that the girl who won The Ugliest Pig Contest at the prom fifteen years ago, be asked to preside over the pig roast tomorrow ..."

A few people laughed, but mostly, the smiles vanished.

"That's the problem with pranks," Hilda continued, "you can never be certain of the outcome . . ."

The room was deadly quiet.

"I'll deliver this tiara, and these roses, personally . . . you see, I'm not Hilda. I'm Linnea. And before my elective surgery two years ago, my name was Lenny."

Hilda sat in a wheel chair by the window in her room at Fairview Nursing Home. Beyond the window was a breathtaking view of colorful flower gardens, rolling green hills and a sky as blue as a robin's egg. But she did not see the scenery, her eyes remaining placid and dead—nor did she appreciate its beauty, for her mind was less than a child's.

"How is she doing today?" Linnea asked the nurse, a matronly woman with a kind face. They stood just outside the doorway.

Linnea had long ago stopped inquiring if her cousin's condition had improved since the attempted suicide; there was no reversing brain damage caused by carbon monoxide poisoning.

"She's been a little restless," the nurse answered. "I can't help but think it's because you've been away."

The nurse looked at the bouquet of roses and the tiara Linnea held in her hands. "She can keep the flowers," the nurse instructed, "but after you've gone, we'll have to take away the crown. I'm afraid one of our more agile guests might 'borrow' it. You understand."

Linnea nodded.

"We'll hold it in the office."

The nurse turned and left.

Linnea entered the room. "Hello, Hilda," she said softly, gently touching her cousin's arm.

The woman's body jerked a little, and the pupils of her eyes moved back and forth, like an infant's trying to make sense of its world.

Linnea sat in a nearby chair.

The afternoon sun streaming in the window moved in a slow arc across the room, as Linnea spoke in a soothing voice, telling her cousin all about the re-union.

Finally, Linnea stood and placed the roses in her cousin's lap, and the tiara on the woman's head. She bent and kissed her.

In the parking lot, Linnea leaned against the steering wheel of her car and wept.

Then she wiped the tears from her face with the back of her hand, and started the car.

"Rock 'n roll radio! Here's a disco blast from the past that will take you back, baby, to nineteen seventy-eight ..."

She wheeled the Porsche into the street. ... *I will survive . . .*

Inconvenience Store a Ms. Tree story

My pregnancy was pretty much uneventful, with the exception of the hostage situation.

I was in my seventh month and still going into my office in the Loop—Tree Investigations, Inc.—and had been working more like the CEO I was supposed to be, rather than field agent I preferred to be.

"You know, Michael," Dan Green said, one hand leaning against my desk, "you don't have to be here. You can go home and relax . . . put your feet up . . ."

"Not without help," I said, smiling a little.

Dan, a slender handsome blonde in his late twenties, had a hook for his left hand and one of his eyes was glass—souvenirs of a dispute with the crime family responsible for the death of my husband, whose name was also Michael Tree. When Mike died and

I took over the agency, I didn't even have to change the lettering on the office door.

"I may be big as a horse," I said, "but I feel great. It's this desk work that's getting me down ... all this damn peace and quiet."

His slightly scarred face broke into a grin and he shook his head, saying, "You're incorrigible."

"Did you scope out the Bandag account?"

He nodded. "It's a plumb. We can sub-contract the day-to-day security and still get rich off the deal."

"What does Roger think?"

Roger Freemont was the third partner in Tree Investigations. My late husband's partner on the force, Roger—balding, brawny, bespectacled, pushing fifty—was the company conservative, our voice of reason.

"I think," Roger said, sticking his shiny head in my door, "we should add staff. Hell with sub-contracting. Let's make *all* the money."

"Spoken like a true Republican," Dan said.

"When we do have to give Bandag our bid?" I asked.

"Monday."

It was Friday.

"You want to hit the computer over the weekend, Roger," I asked, "and make some money comparisons?"

"Sure," he said, sounding almost eager.

"You *are* a Republican," Dan smirked.

"Do it, then," I said. It was four-thirty. "Me, I'm going home . . . well, first I'm going to *pee* and then I'm going home."

"Thanks for sharing," Roger said.

I bid a pleasant weekend to my secretary Effie and to our receptionist Diane, walking through our modern glass-and-ferns office area on surprisingly springy steps. I may have looked like I was trying to smuggle a marijuana-stuffed beach ball across the border, but I felt lighter than air.

That evening, in the masculine-looking apartment that had been my husband's, as I sat on the couch watching a rental video of "Basic Instinct," wondering how anything could be so supremely stupid, chewing on the crust of a Tombstone pizza courtesy of my microwave, I felt an ache in the small of my back (and my back was the only part of me that was small, these days) that might have been a bullet.

"You need exercise, lady," I said to myself (not to Sharon Stone, who was changing her clothes for the umpteenth time on the TV screen), and hauled my butt off the cushions, and stood and held my back with my hands. And groaned.

I glanced toward a window. It was a cool, fall evening out there; even with my baggy woolen blue sweater and stretch pants, I'd need a jacket. I ran a brush through the mop of my brunette hair, and had lipstick poised for application when I sneered at myself in the mirror, slung my purse on its strap over my shoulder, and said, "Fuck it."

When my late husband moved into this side-street two-flat a dozen years ago, Lakeview was a blue-collar neighborhood; now it was Yuppies and gays—safe, as Chicago neighborhoods go. Last year there were only nine murders.

Nonetheless, I was, of course, packing. I'm always reading that "real-life private eyes" don't really carry a weapon. Considering that the mob murdered my husband ten years ago, and that I've lived through perhaps half a dozen attempts on my own life, I'm content to be armed and imaginary.

If you're wondering how I could be pregnant when my husband died a decade ago, I assure you the conception was not immaculate. Suffice to say an old flame flared up, some satisfying if unsafe sex followed, but the relationship didn't last. At an age closer to forty than thirty, however, my biological clock ticking like a time bomb, I decided to keep the child. Ultrasound said a girl was on the way.

The cool breeze whispering through the trees lining the narrow parked-car choked street was soothing, and Friday night or not, the world seemed deserted. It was just after ten, and too late for people to be leaving, and too early for them to be getting home. I walked quickly, getting the spring back in my step, and the kink out of my low back.

Then I had to pee.

It was closer to walk to the Ashland Mini-Mart than back home. Besides, I could use some of Jon's baklava and maybe a can of sardines. Yeah—that sounded *great.* .

A corner storefront on Ashland and an east-west side street, the Mini-Mart was evenly divided between groceries (including fresh fruits and vegetables—typical for Greek proprietors) and liquor. Three of their four coolers were beer and wine.

The well-lighted mart didn't have the modern look of a 7-11; the floor was waxy wooden slats, the ceiling high with rococo trim. You could still squint and imagine the mom-and-pop corner grocery this had been in the 1950s.

"Hey, Ms. Tree," Jon's son Peter said; the dark young skinny handsome kid, in his early twenties, white shirt, black pants, frequently took the all-night shift in this family business. "Pop'll be sorry he missed you. You come for your baklava and sardines fix again?"

"You bet. But can I use your employees-only John? If not, the world's gonna think my water broke."

He grinned and shook his head. "You're a riot, Ms. Tree. Go for it—you know where it is."

I walked back around the counter, saying, "Busy night?"

"So-so. Friday, you always sell plenty of beer and wine coolers. And *lots* of lottery tickets. Payday, and everybody wants that ten-million jackpot."

"Me too. I never buy lottery tickets, but I figure my odds of winning are about the same."

Then I pushed through the swinging stockroom door and shut myself in the bathroom—the lock was broken, but niceties were not a priority—and enjoyed my twelfth or maybe twentieth urination of the day. Impending motherhood is such a spiritual, uplifting experience.

I was still sitting there when the door opened and I looked up, startled, to see my wide-eyed expression reflected in the shiny badge of a potbellied blue-uniformed policeman. His metallic nametag said HALLORAN.

"Sorry, lady," he said, and flashed a pleasant if yellow grin, and shut the door.

A minute or so later, I eased the door open and he was standing right there, staring right in my face—a patrolman in his fifties with the yellow-white hair and red-splotchy complexion of an aging Irish beat cop.

He backed up a step, chuckled gruffly. "Hey, I'm awful sorry. Didn't mean to embarrass you, mother."

"You did give me a start, officer."

He touched his generous belly. "Over anxious. Got me a bad case of the trots."

As he was closing himself inside the John, trots or not, he paused to ask, "When's the little one due?"

"Couple months."

"God bless you both. Shit!" He clutched his belly, shut the door, and, presumably, was as good as his word.

I smiled, shook my head, and coming around the counter asked Peter why he hadn't told the cop the John was in use.

"I was busy with a customer," Peter said, and indeed a guy in a down-filled jacket and plaid hunter's cap was hunkered over the counter, scratching his lottery tickets with the edge of a quarter. "Cops around here don't bother asking—they just go around and help themselves."

"No harm done," I muttered, and headed down one of the four aisles to find my can of sardines.

I was plucking it off the shelf when a harried woman of thirty or so in a tan London Fog raincoat and heels rushed in with a young girl of perhaps seven at her side in a tutu, white leggings and Reeboks, a light jacket over the girl's shoulders. The mother's heels clicked as she went over to a cooler for some milk. The child, blond, stood looking at my pregnancy with wide prairie-sky blue eyes in the midst of an angelic countenance.

"You're going to be a mommy," the little girl said.

"That's right, honey. Recital?"

She nodded. "I'm a ballerina."

The mother, with a jug of 2% milk in hand, was at the counter, speaking to Peter, crossly, even though Peter was in the process of paying off an instant win to the guy in the plaid hat.

"No butter? No eggs?"

"We're out of both, ma'am. Till Monday."

"That's ridiculous! How am I supposed to make breakfast in the morning? Do you have any breakfast rolls?"

The guy in the plaid cap was giving the five bucks he'd won back to Peter in exchange for five more tickets.

"No, and we're out of bread, too. There's some muffin mix in aisle two."

"How do I make that without eggs? You oughta call this an inconvenience store!"

I was at the counter now, with my can of sardines; the woman was between me and the plastic-lidded tray of baklava.

"There's a big mini-mart on Southport," I said. "They have everything."

She glanced over her shoulder at me and pursed her lips in contempt; she was blonde but not as pretty as her daughter— not frowning, anyway. "That's out of my way, thank you very much."

I shrugged. "You're welcome."

"Mommy!" the little girl called, from a nearby aisle. "They have Pop Tarts! Let's have Pop Tarts for breakfast."

Her mother sighed. "Amy, put those down."

Amy, delighted with her Pop Tart discovery (Strawberry), twirled in the aisle, a ballerina in Reeboks. "No, Mommy, I love Pop Tarts! Let's have Pop Tarts!"

The mother joined the daughter and began scolding her, though the little girl didn't seem to be paying much attention. Nor did she seem to be putting the Pop Tarts back.

Peter grinned, teeth white in his dark face; he was a handsome devil. "Two baklava tonight, Ms. Tree?"

The guy in the hunter's cap sighed—none of his five lottery tickets had been worth ten million dollars, or five dollars, either. He trudged out wearily.

"Just one," I said, lifting the lid, helping myself to

one of the pastries in its paper shell. "Don't want me to get fat, now, do you?"

Peter laughed and handed me a small brown paper sack, which I was placing the baklava in when two white boys in ski masks came in, one of them holding a garbage bag open, the other waving a big revolver.

"All your money in the bag, greaseball," the one with the revolver said to Peter.

"Now!" added the other one.

They were skinny, wearing Cubs jackets over heavy metal T-shirts; they had on worn, torn jeans, and Nike pumps that looked like spaceman shoes. The one with the gun was taller—or maybe the gun just made him seem taller.

"Take it easy," Peter said, as he opened his register.

"We'll take it easy, all right!" the one holding the bag said, horse-laughing at his own remarkable wit. His voice was thin, whiny.

I thought about the gun inside the purse over my shoulder, but then I thought about the mother and her daughter a few feet away, and I thought about the child in my belly, and I just stood there while Peter piled cash on the counter and the shorter of the pair used his whole arm to push it into the garbage bag.

Then I heard the sound of a flushing toilet and thought, *Oh shit,* but Halloran was pushing the stockroom door open and coming out and the smile on his mottled Irish face had only barely dissolved into a scowl when the three bullets slammed into his blue shirt and sent him back through the swinging door, on his back.

"You fuckin' killed him, man!" the one holding the bag said.

"Shit," the one with the smoking gun said.

The other one dropped the garbage bag to the slatted-wood floor, where money spilled as easily as blood just had, and he pulled a small nickel-plated revolver out of his waistband; he held it in an unsteady fist.

"A cop," he said, brandishing the gun at his taller partner. "You fuckin' killed a fuckin' cop!"

The swinging door waved at us half-heartedly; it was only a three-quarter affair, with space at top, and bottom, with Halloran's dead feet sticking out below.

The two faced each other, guns in hand. For a moment I thought they were going to save society the trouble; then movement behind him caught the corner of the taller one's eye.

"Jesus!" he said, turning, and he fired again, at a blue shape at the door of the mini-mart, and glass made brittle thunder as it shattered and rained to the pavement, and somebody out there yelled, "Judas Priest!" and Peter ducked down behind his counter, and I did the same on the other side, and the ski-masked pair took cover in an aisle.

Cool evening air and street sounds rushed in from where the glass of the door used to be. "Who the hell was that?" the smaller one said, as they cowered in the aisle next to where I stood.

"Must be the dead pig's partner! Shit ..."

My fingers unclasped my handbag. To my left,

down the next aisle, the mother and her little ballerina cowered together, sitting half-sprawled on the wood floor, the mother looking nearer tears and hysteria than the oddly placid little girl.

From outside a gruff male voice yelled: "Throw out your guns! Walk out slow—hands high!"

"It *is* another cop—what do we do?" the smaller one asked desperately.

"Grab that pregnant bitch!" the taller one said.

The little guy came at me, fast, and I pushed my purse behind the ILLINOIS LOTTERY sign on Peter's counter, back down behind which Peter was looking up with wide-eyed terror.

A gun was in my back and the smaller guy was behind me, as if hiding there; he had room. Still hunkered down in the aisle, his partner yelled out, "We got *people* in here!"

"We got *police* out here!" the gruff voice shouted.

I could see, through the window, between neon beer signs and homemade butcher-paper sale signs, the head of the cop bobbing up behind a car he was using as a barrier; a glint winked off his revolver, as it caught street lights. Sirens were faint cries that were turning into screams; Halloran's partner would not be alone, long.

The little one pulled me by the arm into the aisle with his partner, and down, into a crouching position. I almost fell, but managed to keep my balance.

"Why the fuck did that other cop take so long to come in? If they're partners . . . Jesus!" The taller one remained hunered down, the gun in his hand steadier than that in his pal's.

Peter's voice, as if a ventriloquist's, came from behind the counter: "They always park in the alley but usually come in together. I don't know why he dropped Halloran off, first."

"He had the trots," I said.

"What?" the little guy behind me asked, as if surprised I could talk.

"The runs. Diarrhea."

"Ain't that the shits," the hunkered-down leader said, with no irony. Then thought glimmered in his eyes. "Go check the back, Bud."

"I thought you said no *names,* Frank," Bud said contemptuously. *"Duh!"*

Frank pulled off his ski mask; he was hatchet-faced, pockmarked, with dead gray eyes and wheat-color hair that covered his ears.

"They got us pinned in here," Frank said glumly. "We're gonna have a hostage situation soon. They'll know who we are, all right."

"I told .you we shoulda stole a car," Bud said, shaking his head even as he pulled off his ski mask.

He was round-faced, an odd shape to top such a skinny frame. His head was almost shaved—black five o'clock shadow covering his skull, skinhead style. His acne hadn't turned to pockmarks yet, and his brown eyes were alive, in a stupid sort of way, under heavy eyebrows.

They were kids—just kids, maybe seventeen,

eighteen at most. But for street kids, into drugs, as I assumed they were, that was plenty old. Ancient, in some circles.

Frank pointed his gun at Bud, gesturing as if it were a finger. "Check out the back door. If it looks clear, maybe we can make a break for it, 'fore those other cops get dug in."

The loudness of the sirens made that unlikely, but Bud scrambled off to the backroom, pushing open the door, stepping around Halloran; then the door swung shut, swaying as Halloran's feet disappeared, Bud pulling him out of the way.

"You left your car running?" I asked Frank. "Out front?"

"Yeah," Frank said, wincing with irritation. Hostages weren't supposed to talk: they were supposed to be quiet and scared.

I said, "You thought it'd still be waiting for you? In Chicago?"

"We left it locked."

"You left your car out front, locked, with the motor running? No wonder you gave up on keeping your identities from the cops."

"Shut up, lady."

"Can I sit?"

"Huh?"

"Can I sit? Pregnant women can't crouch long, you know."

"Sit. Sit! And shut the fuck up!"

I sat, my swollen, stretch-pants-covered legs

angling out before me like I was inviting somebody to make a wish. I could hear whimpering in the adjacent aisle, but I couldn't tell if it was the mother or the little ballerina. My purse, nestled behind the ILLINOIS LOTTERY display, beckoned me; but I couldn't come.

Two explosions echoed from the backroom— gunshots— following by a clanging sound, and Bud saying, "Shit!" again and again, at varying volumes, with varying inflections.

Frank sat up, neck straining like a turtle having a look around; the sound of scraping, wood against concrete, sang from the back room.

Cueball Bud came running out, saying, "Cops back there already!"

And, eyes wild in his round face, he crawled on his hands and knees over to join his partner and me in the nearby aisle, the shiny little revolver in one hand, like a child's toy.

"Cops everywhere," he said breathlessly.

"Can they get in?"

"No. Windows are barred back there and the door's steel; I bolted it up, and blocked it with some crates just to make sure. They ain't gettin' in."

"Like you're not getting out," I said.

Round-faced Bud looked at me astounded. "Who the fuck asked you, fatso?"

I shrugged. "Just thought you better face facts."

Hatchet-faced Frank said, "Such as?"

"Such as you're in the midst of a full-blown

hostage crisis." I leaned out in the aisle, nodded toward the street, where the blue revolving lights of several cop cars cut surrealistic paths in the night, and a big Winnebago-style vehicle was rolling in. "Take a look."

Frank and Bud glanced above a row of corn flakes boxes to have a peek. "What the hell's that?" Frank asked.

"That," I said, "is a Mobile Command Unit. Before long they'll be calling you on the phone from there— to start negotiations."

"Negotiations," Bud said stupidly, eyes tight.

I nodded. "So you fellas better decide what you want."

"I just want outa here, Frank!" Bud said.

"It's not that simple," I said.

"What do you know, you fat cow!" Bud shouted, waving his shiny gun at me.

"Play your cards right," I said, "you can trade us for your freedom."

"She's right," Frank said thoughtfully.

"Well, I'm sicka hearin' her voice!" Bud said.

Frank thought about that, too, but his expression turned darker. "You know . . . me, too. Get up and go into the next aisle, mommy—keep that brat and her old lady company."

"You mind if I take a bathroom break first?" I asked.

"You gotta be kidding," Frank said.

"I'm pregnant. I pee a lot. Excuse me for living."

"I can do somethin' about that," Bud said with a sneer.

I smirked, then gestured with two open hands. "What say, boys? To pee or not to pee? That is the question."

They just looked at me stupidly. I'm so frequently too hip for the room.

"Go ahead," Frank said.

"But keep your fat ass away from that back door!" Bud blurted. "If I hear ya movin' those crates, I'll put a bullet in that belly and kill the both of you!"

I hauled myself up. "And here I was thinking of asking you to be the godfather."

In the backroom, I could see that the pile of crates and boxes blocking the door were indeed something I couldn't move without getting caught at it—even if I hadn't been pregnant. Kneeling, I checked Halloran; he was dead, all right— on his back, an angled smeary stripe of red on the concrete indicating how he'd been dragged. Three bloody scorched wounds on his chest, poor bastard—I closed his eyes for him. Wished him God speed. His holster was empty; apparently Bud had taken Halloran's piece, though I hadn't noticed him having it—probably stuck under his Cubby coat. The officer's nightstick, however, was still there. I plucked it from his belt, took it with me into the bathroom, where I again urinated (I hadn't been lying about the need), even as I stuck the baton up my sweater sleeve, holding its tip in the heel of my hand.

Peter was sitting behind the counter; he gave me a pitiful look, and I whispered from the doorway, "Don't you have a gun back there?"

And he shook his head no, looking ashamed.

He shouldn't have, really: half the merchants who trade shots with stick-up men wind up dead. A fascinating statistic that didn't mean diddly right now.

I came out of the backroom, and around the counter; near the LOTTERY sign, where my purse was tucked, I paused. Frank noticed me.

"Get back over in that other aisle," he said, "and keep your big fat trap *shut.*"

I shrugged a response and left my purse where it was. Just didn't want to take the chance.

I joined the mother in their aisle; it smelled of chemicals there and I glanced at the shelves and smiled. Then I sat next to the woman, who was huddled with her daughter, who clung to her mutely. The mother's eyes were brimming with tears. She was stroking her daughter's hair.

I sat. Legs stretched out before me.

The woman whispered harshly. "How can you talk to them?"

I shrugged.

"Just leave them alone!" the woman whispered. "Don't say anything to them—you just make them mad!"

Frank's voice called, "Shut up over there!"

As if in response, a grating loud voice, courtesy of a bullhorn, said, *"Send the people out!"*

"Fuck you!" Bud called.

I withdrew the late Halloran's nightstick from my sweater sleeve. The mother look at me, and it, startled.

"What are you. . ."

I shushed her with a finger to my lips as I placed the baton on a shelf behind me, amid some bathroom supplies.

The bullhorn was barking: *"You boys are going to have a world of trouble if you harm those people. Now, send them out, slowly ..."*

Frank didn't bother to reply. But to Bud he said, bitterly, "World of trouble. We shot a cop. How the fuck can you get in more trouble than that?"

"You shot a cop," Bud reminded him.

"You're as dirty as me. Felony murder. We'll both go down."

"You gotta deal us outa here, Frank!"

I lifted a bottle of liquid drain cleaner off the shelf. Read the directions; savored the poetry of its warnings . .. "poison" . . . "burns on contact" . . . "harmful to eyes" . . .

The woman touched my arm; squeezed hard. She looked at me with wet, hard eyes and shook her head *no,* furiously.

"Don't you risk my child's life," she whispered.

"I have a child at stake, too," I whispered back.

"I said, *shut-up* over there!" Frank almost screamed.

The phone rang and everybody jumped. Me, too. Even Peter—I saw his head bob up.

On his hands and knees, the big revolver in hand, Frank scrambled over behind the counter, as the phone rang and rang, and he plucked the receiver off and was down behind the counter, where Peter was, as he answered.

"How many? I'll tell you how many. We got a greaseball clerk, a mommy and her little girl, and a pregnant woman. How do you *like* our little party?"

I unscrewed the cap of the liquid drain cleaner; sniffed its harsh bouquet . . .

"What do we *want?* We want a jet! We want a car, and a police escort to O'Hare ..."

I could guarantee them the police escort.

"... and then we want the biggest goddamn jet they got! . . . Where?" Frank paused, apparently thinking, then his voice called to Bud: "Where do *you* want to go?"

Bud seemed to think for a while, then his voice called: "Vegas?"

"You moron! Somewhere foreign! Some *other* country!"

"Alaska?"

I would have laughed, except the frozen little ballerina whose head was in her mother's lap was looking at me with eyes that could not widen enough to express her fear.

Frank was saying into the phone, "Never mind where. Just have plenty of fuckin' fuel onboard. We'll tell the pilot where to take us . . . and we want money, too! . . . How *much?*"

Frank, despite the lousy luck of his last attempt, called out to Bud for an opinion. "How much dough should we ask for?"

Bud didn't hesitate; he knew just the amount. "Ten million bucks!"

"Get real," Frank snorted. Back on the phone, he said, "A million in cash. Small unmarked bills—nothin' bigger than a fifty."

Shrewd boy, this Frank.

"Okay," he was saying. "Call back when you got an answer for me."

Frank's hand reached up and slammed the receiver on the hook.

I figured drugs were why this skinny pair was after the money—all but forgotten in the garbage bag, bills spilled out on the floor over by the counter, like discarded lottery winnings. But like a lot of addicts, for whom stealing was a job, they had apparently planned ahead, not waiting till they needed a fix, not wanting to go out on a heist in that condition.

Still, sometimes it pays to needle a junkie.

"You boys might be here a while," I said to Frank as he crawled by. "Lining up that jet's gonna take time. Getting the mayor to approve all that dough—and hauling some banker out of his country club dance to unlock a vault. We could be here for hours."

Bud, from the next aisle, said, "Frank—I'm gonna need a shot before that!"

"Shut up, Bud," Frank said; but he was frozen on his hands and knees, looking at me, thinking over what I said. "You got a point, lady?"

"Frank!" Bud yelled. "We can't wait that long. I'm gonna need a shot! Ask for less money. Get fifty K or something."

"Shut up! Lady—what's your fuckin' point?"

"Let this mother and her daughter go," I said. "It'll buy you some good will, and show the authorities you're reasonable guys. Besides . . . you got me—a pregnant woman—what better hostage could you ask for? Nobody's going to shoot at you guys if you're walking behind a pregnant woman."

Frank's eyes were turning to slits as he smiled. "You could be right about that last part. I don't know about giving up no hostages, though ..."

"You'll have the cashier," I said, nodding toward the counter, where my purse sat, a million miles away, "and me. One hostage for you, one for your friend. You can take us with you in the car to O'Hare—which you can't do with mommy and her ballerina, here. Let 'em go. You'll be popular."

"Don't listen to her, Frank!" Bud whined. "I don't trust her!"

Frank was studying me, like a lab tech studying a slide. "Who *are* you, lady? Why do you know so much? Why are you so fuckin' chilled out?"

I shrugged. "My late husband was a cop."

That seemed to satisfy him.

"Let the mother and her kid go," I said. "You don't need them. You didn't mean for this to happen, did you, Frank? This is just something that got out of hand ... let 'em go."

Bud was sticking his head around the aisle to watch this conversation. He was on the floor on his stomach. He looked like a bug with a big head.

He said, "Don't do it, Frank."

Frank was thinking it over. Something had flickered in his eyes—traces of humanity, maybe?—as I'd spoken. Was he looking past me at the woman hugging her child? Was there something human or humane in this lost teenager's white trash past?

He swallowed and said, "She's right."

"Frank ..."

"Shut the fuck up, Bud. There's only two of us ... we can manage better with just her and the guy back of the counter."

"O . . . okay, Frank," Bud said, half-sticking out in the aisle on his belly. "But let's shake it . . . I'm gonna need a fuckin' shot before long!"

Bud did seem to be getting the shakes, and it wasn't fear alone. The little hop-head, by his own admission, slammed his drugs—injected them—as opposed to smoking or snorting, which meant time was going to catch up with him.

Suddenly Frank yelled; it startled the mother, and the child, and me, too. Peter probably peed his pants.

"Hold your fire!" Frank was calling to the cops outside. "We're sendin' out some hostages!"

Frank crawled back around the counter, so he could get a better vantage point I guess—and it did give him an angle where the cops outside couldn't see him, or get a bead on him—and he said to the mother, "Okay, you and your little girl get up and walk out. Real slow."

The mother allowed herself the briefest smile, and glanced at me with an expression that might have been of thanks, as she helped her child up. She could spare me any gratitude, now or later: I hadn't done this for her.

The little ballerina hung onto her mother's waist as they slowly walked out of the aisle and past the counter where Frank held a gun on them. They walked by the aisle where Bud was taking cover, up to the front of the mini-mart where the mother gingerly opened the metal framework of the shot-out glass door and they were outside.

With a sigh of relief, I watched from my aisle, where I sat leaning back against the shelf of bathroom supplies; I could see the mother and daughter as two cops rushed to help them past the parked cars toward the street filled with squads, moving them toward the Winnebago command center.

"That was the right thing to do," I told Frank.

"Shut up," he said, and he moved out from around the counter.

As he walked past me, I hurled Halloran's nightstick under his feet, and Frank's Nikes hit the baton and he did a crazy, log-rolling dance, and as the kid was twisting around, I splashed the liquid drain cleaner in his face and he screamed and I splashed it again and he screamed again.

"Frank!" Bud yelled. "Jesus, Frank!"

He landed hard, on his back, his hands clawing his face and eyes, the big revolver dropping to the slick wood floor and spinning, like a top, till it came to a rest at my feet. I scooped it up, as Frank continued to scream and Bud yelled incoherently.

Before the little hop-head could get his wits about him, I came around the other side, up the other end of the aisle, behind him, where he continued to crouch, and cower, the nickel-plated revolver in hand, watching his pal wriggle and writhe like an insect under a pin.

Bud's incoherent yelling stopped when I put the nose of Frank's revolver in the back of his stubbly head and told him to stand up.

"You bitch! What did you do to Frank?"

Frank was still screaming.

"Cleaned his drain." I reached my left hand past his left ear; held the hand open, palm up. "Let's have the gun, Bud. Give it to Mommy ..."

He placed the shiny revolver in my palm; swore at me some more.

"March up by the counter. By where your friend Frank is. By the way, we ought to hurry—if he doesn't get some first-aid soon, he's going to need a cane and a guide dog."

"You're evil!"

"I guess you'd know. Move it."

He did.

The phone was ringing. The cops were wondering was going on in here; through the neon beer-ad and butcher-paper sign cluttered window, vision was only so-so.

"Get that, would you, Peter?" I asked.

Peter's dark face with its wide eye peered over the

edge and the fingers of both hands were pressed against the countertop. He looked like Kilroy Was Here.

"Stand up," I said. "Situation's under control."

I placed Bud's shiny nickel-plated revolver on the counter. Frank was on the floor, on his side, in fetal position, his hands covering his face, and he wasn't screaming now, whimpering instead, saying something about "burning." Bud was standing next to him, looking down like he wished he could help.

Peter, who had answered the phone, covered the receiver and said to me, "They want to know what's going on."

"Tell them to come in and see for themselves," I said, and then I thought about the reporters who'd soon be swarming, and I was rustling around in my purse for my lipstick when Bud pulled Halloran's gun out from under his Cubs jacket.

"I'm going to kill you, you fat bitch," the round-faced little junkie said, his saliva making a mist in the air.

I shot him through the bottom of my handbag and the top of his head.

He flew back, flopping next to Frank, leaving a mist of blood this time, and his body made a squishing sound when he landed on the brain matter he'd spilled. They were both on their backs, but Frank didn't seem to notice the company. He was busy.

The garbage bag of spilled money was nearby—a cheap irony, but it couldn't be helped.

Peter's mouth had dropped open.

I shrugged. "He said he needed a shot."

One of the first cops on the scene, in the aftermath, was Lt. Valer, a thirty-something black good-looking homicide detective I'd known for years.

"How did you manage to be here when all this happened?" he asked. His smile was a wry dimple in one cheek.

"Baby needs baklava," I said, and put two in my little paper sack. Not to mention sardines.

Peter wasn't behind the counter anymore; he'd gone somewhere to have a minor nervous breakdown, I guess. I thought about leaving him some money for the pastries, then decided I'd earned them.

"Excuse me a moment, Rafe? I have to use the John."

Halloran's body had already been moved; lab techs were at work back there.

"You aren't going to touch anything, are you?" one of them said, a snotty redheaded woman in her twenties.

"Well, I might," I said, and closed myself in the John.

When I came out from the backroom, Rafe said, "That punk . . . Frank? . . . he's going to be all right. Suffered some burns, but his eyesight won't be permanently affected."

"Swell," I said. "Those two got rap sheets from here to Wilmette. But they're just kids. Both of 'em under eighteen."

"Pity."

His smile disappeared; his eyes narrowed judg-mentally. "You don't care? It doesn't bother you, killing a kid like that?"

"He was pointing a murdered cop's gun at me, Rafe. What would you have done? Burp him?"

He sighed. "You got a point. But you better brace yourself—you're going to take some heat."

I laughed. "It's not politically correct for a hostage to fight back?"

Rafe's wry dimple reappeared in the other cheek. "You're not the average hostage. This won't be the first time you've made the papers."

"It won't be the last, either."

"Yeah?"

"Watch the birth announcements," I said, and took my bag of baklava, and sardines, and walked home.

Seeing Red

It seemed to Deborah that every cell in her bloated body was about to burst. If her period didn't start soon, she was going to *kill* somebody!

She sat back in the leather chair and tugged viciously through her red silk dress at the tight elastic waistband on her pantyhose. Then she leaned forward and opened the top right drawer of her mahogany desk and pulled out a pair of long, silver scissors, which she dropped into her open purse on the floor by her feet. She got up from the desk, taking the purse, and walked briskly, tensely, to the closed office door. But as soon as she opened it, she forced her body to relax, and changed her cross expression to one of pleasantry.

"I'll be back in a minute, Shirley," she said sweetly to the secretary who sat behind a desk in the outer room.

The secretary, a rather homely woman with short hair and big, round glasses, looked up briefly from what she was doing. "Yes, Ms. Nova," she said, then returned to her work.

Deborah walked down the plush-carpeted corridor toward the executive's washroom, nodding and smiling at a few people along the way . . . but once inside the bathroom, behind its thick bronze-colored door, her expression changed back to one of annoyance as she marched across the marble floor, her high-heeled shoes click, click, clicking.

She threw open a stall, entered, then slammed it shut.

She got out the scissors and yanked up her dress.

"I'd like to get my hands on the son-of-a-bitch that designed these pantyhose," she snarled, sliding one of the silver blades down between her stomach and the hose, cutting away savagely at the binding band. "You can *bet* it wasn't a *woman!*"

Her discomfort somewhat relieved, she held up the scissors in front of her face. Snip! snip! went the blades, glinting in the overhead light. "I'd take *this* to his ..."

Water ran in a sink.

Composing herself, Deborah exited the stall.

A younger woman in a dark tailored suit stood at one of the shell-shaped basins washing her hands. Her blonde hair was pulled back from an attractive face and held at the nape of her neck by an ornate barrette. Expensive earrings clung to delicate ears.

"Hello, Deborah," the woman said.

"Heather," Deborah responded, noncommittally. She moved to an adjacent basin and turned the crystal knobs on the faucet. The two women, standing side by side, eyed each other in the mirror. They looked similar, despite their difference in age, which was almost a decade.

Deborah thought she herself looked better.

"I need your help," Heather said, breaking the silence.

Deborah, wiping her hands on a paper towel, turned to face the woman. "Oh?" she smiled.

"I understand the second chair hasn't been filled yet for the Owens case. I'd like a shot at it."

Deborah continued to smile.

"I would do a good job," the woman said confidently.

"Yes, I believe you could."

"Then you'll recommend me?"

Deborah, finished with the towel, wadded it up. "Certainly, I will," she said.

Heather smiled and thanked Deborah, and left the bathroom.

Deborah stared after the woman, nerves strung out as tight as pantyhose in a strangler's hands.

"Certainly, I will," she repeated. *"Not!"*

She reared back and threw the wadded-up paper towel angrily at the wastebasket. "I didn't claw my way up this good-old-boy network just to hand *you* a plum position on a silver platter!"

Deborah turned back to the mirror and got lipstick out of her purse and applied the blood-red color to her collagen-injected lips.

"You'd better go home," she warned her reflection, "before you blow it. Remember Laura."

The thought of that woman, and what happened to her, brought a new rush of heat to Deborah's already flushed cheeks.

It was fifteen years ago that Deborah, fresh out of law school and new to the firm, was an associate to Laura. The woman was her idol, a Harvard graduate of distinction, a talented and brilliant lawyer . . . and the first female certain to become a partner in this all-boys-club.

But it never came to pass. Because Laura made a fatal mistake one day: she showed some emotion.

Mr. Laroma, a senior partner in a pin-striped suit, looked at Laura from across the conference table and smirked, "Maybe we should discuss this later . . . *after* you've had your period."

Though a stunned silence hung in the air, Deborah would never forget the collective look on the men's faces: one of masked approval. Laura fled the room, and a short time later, the company.

The incident was a turning point for Deborah; after that, she told herself, she would be a man in drag.

And now, with partnership so close she could almost reach out and touch it, she'd better not show *any* female weakness. Especially hormonal. Deborah walked back to her office.

"If Mr. Laroma should need me," Deborah informed her secretary, "he can reach me at home."

Deborah packed up her briefcase, then took the elevator down to an underground garage where she got in her gray BMW and drove out to the street. After a few blocks, she pulled into a "No Parking" zone in front of a dry-cleaners, got out of the car and entered the store.

A thin young man with a bad case of acne stood behind the counter. She stepped up and set her purse down, then rummaged around in the bag for her dry-cleaning ticket. She stopped, realizing she'd left it at home.

"Damn," she said irritably. "I don't have the ticket.. . but it's a white silk blouse and blue suit."

"Sorry," the kid said flatly, "I need the ticket."

Deborah softened her expression and voice, "Can't you make an exception?" she asked sweetly.

"Nope. Those are the rules."

Deborah studied him for a moment, then sighed deeply. "And 150 wanted to wear them to the AIDS benefit tonight."

For a second the kid seemed to reconsider. But then he said, again, "I need the ticket."

Deborah slammed both fists on the counter making her purse jump. "Listen, you pimply-faced faggot," she growled, "give me my clothes or I'll ..."

"*I'll* call the cops," he said firmly, and moved toward a nearby phone to make good his threat.

Deborah turned in a huff and stomped out to the

curb where she found a different kind of ticket on the windshield of her car.

She grabbed the pink parking violation, nearly dislocating the wiper, and looked up and down the street. She spotted the policewoman who had given her the ticket. "I *was just* in there a *minute!*" Deborah shouted at her.

The cop ignored Deborah.

So Deborah screamed, "Why don't you get a *real* job!" and tore the ticket into tiny pieces, scattering them to the wind.

She got in her car and, without looking, pulled out from the curb, nearly causing an accident. Brakes squealed as the other motorist honked his horn.

She gave him the finger.

Weaving recklessly in and out of the downtown traffic, Deborah caught the north-bound expressway that would take her out to her home in the suburbs. But before long the expressway slowed, congested with commuters, and Deborah, behind the wheel, fumed, then found some classical music on the radio to calm herself down. But after a while, the violin concerto sounded like fingernails on a blackboard and Deborah shut off the radio with a *click.*

Now the traffic was at a near standstill, and Deborah, crawling past an exit, got off. She'd wait out the rush hour at a nearby mall, and besides, she thought, shopping always made her feel better. And she could use the time to find a present for her mother's birthday—though it didn't matter how carefully Deborah picked out the gift or how expensive it was . . . nothing ever pleased her mother.

It seemed to Deborah that she spent her entire life looking for affection; though she got it, briefly, from her father—until she was eight years old. That's when he left her. He didn't have the decency to wait until she had gone off to school that morning. She stood crying at the window—just a little girl— watching him get in the car with his suitcases. He didn't even look back.

She didn't see or hear from him again until a few years ago. He called her at the office, out of the blue . . . said he was sorry he had dropped out of sight. He'd like to make it up to her. She wanted—so badly—to reach out to him, to know him, to love him. But the little girl wouldn't let her.

She told him to go fuck himself.

Deborah pulled her car into the parking lot of the mall, which was full. She drove around and around looking for a place to park. The third time she passed the empty handicapped spaces up at the front, she complained, "How *many* do they *need?* They get all the breaks!"

Then two heavy-set women in jogging clothes— obviously on their way to use the mall as a track, a trend Deborah hated—stepped out in the cross-walk, and she had to slam on her brakes and let them pass.

She watched the women disdainfully, envisioning elephants, and rolled down her window and hollered, "It's not working!"

Around she drove again, when suddenly, up at the front, and very close to the mall, brake lights went on.

"There *is* a God!" Deborah cried, and zoomed ahead, putting on her turn signal to lay claim to the spot.

Impatiently she tapped her red nails on the steering wheel, waiting for the Chevy truck to back out, its body perched precariously up on big wheels.

"Come on, come *on,*" she muttered. "Show me a jacked-up truck and I'll show you a man who wishes his *dick* were bigger."

Slowly the Chevy backed out and started to leave, but as soon as it did, a black Porsche roared around the corner and stole the parking space.

Behind the wheel of the Porsche was a business-man in a suit. And a smirk on his face.

Shouting a string of obscenities, Deborah explod-ed, slammed her accelerator to the floor and aimed the front of her car for the back of his ass!

*****

Steve was depressed. Up until six months ago—that's when it started—the feeling had been foreign to him.

An outgoing, up-beat, aggressive man, he'd en-joyed a damn near perfect life. Nurturing and support-ive parents, attending the best schools, more friends than he knew what to do with . . . Steve seemed bless-ed from birth. After graduating from college, he had married the prettiest woman on campus, and landed a good job with an insurance company.

Now, fifteen years later, walking out of that company into a cold, gray, overcast day, Steve felt the jaws of depression tighten their grip, pulling him down, down, into a dark abyss out of which he could see no possible escape.

He got into his black Porsche, kicking a small handgun that had slid out from under the front seat; he had bought the weapon last year when there was a rash of smash-and-grab car thieves terrorizing the city.

That's all he needed, he thought, was to shoot himself in the goddamn foot. Shaking his head, he tucked the gun back under the seat, started the car and roared off, catching the south-bound freeway that would head him toward the city to an apartment where he lived alone.

But traffic was snarled, at a near stand-still, giving Steve nothing to do but think. And finally, he allowed something that had been eating away inside of him to gnaw its way out. . .

It was last May when Steve went back to his hometown for his twenty-fifth high school class reunion. His wife, Kathleen, decided not to go; their three kids were busy with their own activities, and she would be needed. And besides, Kathleen had said with a smile, he'd have more fun by himself.

Steve hadn't been back to Iowa since he graduated from high school. Over the years, the tenth, fifteenth, then twentieth class reunion forms found their way to him as he moved around the country for his company. And each time he sat down at his desk and filled out the paper—until he came to the part that asked his occupation. Insurance salesman. Not very befitting to the boy voted most likely to succeed. No, he told himself, until he could write that he was president of the company, he wouldn't attend.

But this time Steve made an exception. He was now a vice-president, with the presidency certain to be his.

The night before he left, he dug out his old high-school yearbook and pored over it, so he would re-member his classmates. Then he got out the booklet that came with his banquet ticket; it told what everyone was presently doing. He studied it, as if there would be an exam, smiling as he did so, until he reached the last page. Fifteen names filled a memorial page. It upset him to know that these people were dead . . .

Yet, it would be *great* to see old friends. Especially Rob. He grinned, thinking of all the rebellious scrapes he and his best friend had gotten into.

Steve shook his head, his smile fading. How could he have lost touch with Rob? They were like brothers, for Christ's sake! He made a promise to himself that at the reunion he would renew that friendship. After all, he thought, looking again at the memorial page, life was just too damn short.

Steve thumbed back through the booklet, and noticed that his old girlfriend, Melissa, listed no spouse . . .

Okay, so he envisioned making it with Melissa. So what. Like no married *woman* ever had thoughts about another man. It was just a harmless fantasy that helped pass the time on his long drive back to Iowa. Yes, he knew he had a great job, a wonderful wife, and three terrific kids. He wasn't *stupid*. And yet, memories of Melissa—a love almost consummated—seemed more and more like unfinished business in his mind.

After arriving in town, Steve checked in to a hotel, taking a suite—in case anyone might want to come back and party. Then he showered and shaved, and carefully combed his recently dyed hair. He put on tight, white Bermuda shorts and a pale yellow polo shirt that showed off his spa-tanned skin. A leather Rolex was strapped to his wrist.

He stood at the mirror—looking more like a thirty-three than forty-three year old man—and, satisfied with his appearance, he left the room, and went out to his Porsche.

Indianola was a small town in a rural community with a population of about ten thousand. Driving around the downtown, which was built in a square around a quaint little park, Steve thought things hadn't changed much in twenty-five years. Oh, sure, there were some new shops, but the old, gothic theater with its great marquee, and Pasquale's Pizzeria—where *everyone* hung out—took him zooming back in time.

Steve felt a lump in his throat.

He turned down a side street and pulled his Porsche into a parking lot next to a big, three-story brown brick building, which was the old YMCA where they used to have sock-hops. Vacant for some time, the reunion committee re-opened it for this Friday night dance—for old time's sake.

Steve parked his car and got out.

As he opened the door to the building, loud talking and laughter floated down from the second floor parlor. He smiled as he climbed the short flight of steps, nervous in a way he hadn't felt since high school.

But when he entered the parlor, he became confused and disoriented, like a kid who'd wandered into the wrong classroom. Looking out over the sea of faces he recognized no one. He must be at the wrong reunion; these people were *old.* And yet, some reached out and grabbed at him and called his name. With a frozen smile he moved through the crowd, as if in a slow-motion picture.

Then behind him he heard a low, soft voice.

Melissa.

He sighed, relieved to know someone, and grinning, he turned.

But the grin collapsed like a fat lady in a folding chair, for Melissa was short and dumpy. Beneath curly gray hair lay a wrinkled face where here and there skin-tags clung like tiny particles of forgotten food. The bright orange dress she wore (Christ on a crutch, why would she want to draw attention to herself?) was shaped like a tent.

Steve's thoughts must have registered on his face, because Melissa had a hurt look on hers. Quickly he turned on the charm and told her how nice it was to see her again and how pretty she looked.

She perked up, and latched onto him, and launched into her life's history since high school . . . which was a *nightmare.* Listening to her babble on and on, Steve never realized it before, but the woman had the IQ of a gerbil! When she started to show him pictures of ugly grandchildren, he got away from her, and moved to the other side of the room.

What *happened?* he thought. Was *this* the generation that was going to change the world? It didn't seem possible! Had they just given the fuck up? Turned into their parents—but *worse?*

Was this *old man* in plaid polyester pants, now boring him to death with talk of aluminum siding, the same Rob from high school? Steve stared at his old friend.

Hello! Hello! Is anybody in there?

Steve fled the parlor, hurrying up a flight of wide, wooden steps that creaked and moaned with their age, and went into the gymnasium where the dance was being held. It was dark in there—mercifully—the only source of light coming from the band on stage, and a large glittering ball that revolved on the ceiling; the ball sent a million white spots swirling around, making it look like the room had some contagious disease. The gym itself was small, just the size of a basketball court with no room for bleachers. Crepe paper hung from corner to corner, while a hundred balloons clung to the walls.

Steve took a chair at one of the long banquet tables, and watched the couples out on the floor, holding each other, dancing to a slow song, seemingly content with their lives. . .

He felt miserable.

Then the band—five guys who were also no spring chickens—began to play a song by the Association he hadn't heard since high school.

. . . *enter the young*. . .

Slowly Steve rose to his feet.

He started to weep.

He bolted from the room and down the wooden steps and out the front door, to his car, where he drove to an all-night liquor store, bought a bottle of bourbon, went back to his hotel room and drank it, until he passed out, on the floor, in his own vomit.

And now, crawling along the expressway, it occurred to Steve—in a revelation—that it was just a few weeks after returning from that class reunion that the anxiety attacks began.

The first one sent him rushing to the emergency room in the middle of the night, certain he was having heart failure. But an EKG and follow-up tests showed nothing was wrong. After that, he suffered them in silence.

The next indignity was Kathleen accusing him of being obsessed with sex. He'd always felt he had a satisfying love life—hell, *better* than satisfying. He was damn lucky to have such a sexy and obliging wife—and with three kids in the house! He supposed he had been hornier than usual—as if in the mass production of his sperm there somehow held the promise of immortality—but he never foresaw the night when, in a tearful confrontation, Kathleen told him she had had enough, and to get it someplace else.

So he did.

Kathleen kicked him out, of course. He couldn't blame her. His life was out of control, like a child's top spinning wildly on a table, heading straight for the edge . . . and he had neither the ability nor the desire to stop it.

Then came the *coup de grace.* Somebody else got to be president of the company. A younger man. Suddenly, as if overnight, Steve was perceived—or so he thought—as "too old." What depressed him more than anything else was knowing the finality of what lay before him: too late to start over with another company, he would go no further up the ladder of success.

Steve needed a fix ... in the form of Jennifer who worked at an Orange Julius at a mall. She was dumb as a post, but young and pretty. And between her creamy white thighs was the only place he could get away from his demons.

He left the crowded expressway, and drove to the mall. He'd treat Jennifer to an expensive dinner, he thought, then she would make him feel better . . . sad pathetic excuse for a man that he was . . .

He smirked, hating himself, and pulled into a parking place. He turned off the engine and was undoing the seatbelt, when a tremendous force from behind drove him into the windshield, his head cracking up against the glass. While he didn't lose consciousness,

Steve was so stunned he remained motionless for a moment, slumped over the steering wheel. Then dazed, his head throbbing, he leaned back against the seat, and saw, in his rearview mirror, the car that hit him roar off. Suddenly he sat up straight, given a jolt of electricity in the form of vengeance, and started his car and took out after the BMW.

He caught up to it, after the fourth stop light, but there was another car between them. He wheeled into a corner gas station, came out the other end and went into the intersection, in front of the BMW, to cut it off; he could not see inside the car's tinted windows.

When the light changed, car horns blared at him blocking the way, and the BMW accelerated, slamming his left backside, spinning him around, leaving him in the dust.

Now nothing mattered to Steve—not his life or the lives of anyone else—in his pursuit of the bastard in the BMW, over curbs and through red lights on their mad race out of the suburbs and into the country.

After a while the BMW swerved off the highway onto a secondary road. On a straightaway, Steve tried to overtake it, but the BMW was just too powerful. He pulled back a bit, saving his engine for the upgrade just ahead as the road began to wind up a steep hill that lead to a quarry.

Was this maniac luring him to some desolate place in order to kill him? Steve wasn't about to wait and find out; he reached under his seat for the gun.

On a curve up the hill he buried his accelerator

on the floor and sped up as close as he could to the other car, rolled down his window and fired. *Blam!* The back window of the BMW exploded, glass shards flying back onto his windshield and hand.

The BMW careened violently to the left and then to the right, skittering along a metal guardrail that bowed out as if it were a rubber band, straining to keep the car from going over the edge of the cliff. The BMW spun around and came to a halt, hung up on the rail.

Steve pulled his Porsche off to the side and waited.

Operating on adrenaline, legs feeling weak, Steve shielded his eyes from the sun that peered out from the clouds, an interested spectator, as he carefully approached the BMW. He yanked open the car door on the driver's side, gun ready to use.

But it didn't seem necessary. A woman in a red dress was slumped over the wheel, blond hair covering her face.

Steve didn't know what to think; he'd expected a man.

Carefully he pushed the woman back against the seat, revealing her face, which he did not recognize. She didn't appear to be badly hurt; the only sign of blood was a thin trickle down her left leg.

Steve relaxed his grip on the gun. Was she someone he picked up in a bar for a one-night stand? he wondered. Was that what this was? Some kind of fatal attraction?

On the front seat, next to the woman, lay a purse, opened. He leaned in, past her, to look for some identification.

His fingers were on a wallet when he felt a burning in his side that made him scream out with pain. He pulled back, out of the car, and saw scissors sticking out of his side.

Now the woman came at him, with a wild look in her eyes, and he brought up his hand with the gun and shot her. The force threw her back on the seat, but after a second she sat up like some superwoman and threw herself on him and they stumbled backward, doing an awkward little dance like a pair of marionettes, and tripped on the mangled guard rail and went over the cliffs edge together in a stunned embrace.

Below, a pair of frightened eyes watched.

He'd been out in the stream, fishing, looking for food to feed his family, when the violence erupted. It forced him back to the bank where he hid in the brush, fearful of repercussions, shivering in his brown fur coat.

After a while, when the sun began to set behind the cliff, its long rays winking goodbye, he ventured out. Cautiously he slid into the stream, and swam toward the humans that lay twisted on the rocks, their limbs entwined like the briar bush he had just crawled out of.

Halfway across, he stopped, sniffing, his head bobbing on the water's surface. He need not go any further: death hung in the air.

He turned and swam downstream a ways, then dove under and entered a hole in the bottom of the bank that then led upward to his house.

Inside the dark, dank chamber, lined with grass, the female muskrat waited; nestled against her warm body were four tiny babies.

He lay protectively next to her and she snuggled up to him. Tomorrow, he would hunt for tadpoles— but further downstream, away from the vile humans. And she would clean the house and take care of the babies . . .

Yes, tomorrow would be another glorious day.

Catgate

Senator Jim Rawson, Democrat, Iowa, 45 years of age, pulled the sleek red sports car over along the edge of the gravel road. Virginia farmland, washed in moonlight, surrounded him, a fertile and yet desolate landscape, serene in its isolation. Not a farmhouse in sight; certainly not a car. And the only other human being present was a dead one.

Vicki.

The busty young woman wore a pink T-shirt and jeans and running shoes—though she was in her late twenties, she might have been a college girl. Her features were cute—big long-lashed eyes (shut now), pert nose, pouty puffy lips. She was slumped against the other window of the Jaguar. He'd have to move her.

Leaving the driver's side door open, Rawson—in

University of Iowa yellow-and-black sweatshirt and black jeans and black leather gloves—came around and carried her from the rider's side of the vehicle. It was as if he were carrying a bride across the threshold, although the only threshold Vicki Petersen had crossed was death's, and she'd done that several hours ago.

Rawson—tall, raw-boned, with blonde-brown hair touched at the temples by distinguished gray—had a Marlboro man look that bode well with his conservative constituency. Iowans rarely voted Democrats to the Senate. Rawson had maintained the office for three terms (with dead-certain re-election coming up next year) by balancing his own slightly left-of-center politics with country charm.

As he gently conveyed the shapely and very dead body of the woman who had been his mistress for three years, he was bitterly aware of his own reputation as a champion of women's rights, a battler for ERA, a vocal defender of Anita Hill. This irony left a bitter taste in his being as he arranged the corpse behind the wheel of the sports car, which had been purchased by him, in cash, with PAC money a little more than a year before.

"I loved you, Vicki," he said, and could hear his voice waver; tears were blurring his vision, if not his mission. "But you betrayed me."

Could she have really believed he would marry her? A Catholic in a predominantly Protestant state, Rawson knew the good people of Iowa would never stand for him divorcing, childless marriage or not, particularly not with a wife who was bedridden back home, wasting away with MS.

And then to threaten him with exposure—"How would you like to see our story on 'A Current Affair,' or maybe 'Hard Copy'? Maybe I could play myself in the TV movie!"— truly contemptible.

You little bitch, he thought, and raised a hand as if to slap her, but the beautiful, eternally slumbering woman behind the wheel was past feeling any such sting, and he immediately felt a flush of shame.

He sighed. A summer breeze riffled a nearby field of wheat, and his own wheat-colored, dead-dry hair. The moon was like a hole punched in a black starless sky, letting in too much light. He looked at his watch, shut the girl's car door with a *thunk* that echoed across the world. Where *was* Edward, anyway?

It was highly unlikely this dead girl would ever come back to haunt him. He knew that. The only nervousness he felt was immediate—once Edward had arrived, and he was back safely in his townhouse on P Street in Georgetown, Jim Rawson would be secure, with his best and only true friend— the big gray mixed-breed cat, Tricky Dick—settled on his lap.

He wondered if Dick would mourn the missing Vicki—the cat and the girl had taken to each other from the start. . . .

A little over ten years ago, Vicki Petersen had been a cheerleader at the University of Iowa, a small-town girl with a big future—until she flunked out in her sophomore year, and found her way to New York, where an acting career seemed to beckon. Naturally top-heavy, her high, soft yet firm silicone-free breasts became tickets to stardom on the strip club circuit.

This had been prior to the more recent influx of upscale topless nightclubs, venues in which she might have made some real money. But a few years ago, stripping was less lucrative, and when Rawson met her in a D.C. bar called the Gentleman's Club, she was at a low ebb.

He had encouraged her to quit her job as a stripper and get back to pursuing her acting career; as a senator, he'd met and maintained personal relationships with any number of Hollywood celebrities and could certainly help her make some connections.

She had been drawn to him immediately, he could tell— after all, not only was he a senator, and as handsome as Robert Redford, but a superstar celebrity back in her home state. Their affair had begun that first night.

Rawson didn't like risking motels—you never knew when some sleazeball reporter was lurking in the bushes, waiting to make Gary Hart out of you—so early on in the relationship he had ensconced the girl in a suite at the Watergate. Irony was second-nature to Rawson, and he relished having his mistress spirited comfortably (and handily) away in the hotel and apartment complex where a break-in had once led to that sleazeball Richard Nixon's downfall. Vicki had been a private person. Her family back in Iowa—farm folk—had been kept in the dark about her stripping career. She would hardly have told them about an affair she was having.

Nor did she have any girlfriends among the strippers on the topless circuit—her aspirations toward acting had made her a snob toward them. They were sluts, tramps, low-lifes; she, on the other hand, was an actress reluctantly taking on this demeaning "role" on her way to a real career on stage or screen.

He knew she had made a few friends with other single women tenants at the Watergate—secretaries and such. But he had been adamant about her not sharing any secrets with them—after all (as he had drilled into her), these were women who swam in the same dirty Washington waters as he, working for this lobbying firm or that Political Action Committee; the wrong word to the right one of them, and he'd be sunk. And, so, he felt confident she'd protected him.

Even if she had mentioned him to a girl friend (and he doubted it), he knew they had never been seen together; no photographs of them, as a couple, existed to become a nasty surprise on the *Enquirer* cover.

She invariably would be picked up by Edward in the limo with its dark windows and brought into the townhouse from a garage in the alley that connected with an underground passageway that connected all of the homes on this block. Only Rawson knew about it, however, and that allowed Edward to bring Miss Petersen into (and out of) the P Street townhouse undetected.

"If people see us together," he would tell her, "it will taint our eventual marriage. When Marge passes away, we'll 'meet' for the 'first time,' and you'll be a Senator's wife with all the respect and attention you deserve." He could see how much she liked the sound of that, and knew she wouldn't risk such a future. But she had grown impatient of late, saying, "That woman is *never* going to die! Divorce her! No one will blame you."

She didn't understand that she was asking him to commit political suicide.

And now, thanks to the cocktail she'd sipped at the town-house, laced with a deadly, tasteless and thankfully painless poison, she had committed literal suicide.

Not intentionally, of course, but the world wouldn't know that. They would find a frustrated would-be actress, and ex-stripper, an empty pill bottle beside her lifeless form, a poor dead girl who wound up along the country roadside in a Jaguar purchased her by some unknown gentleman friend who had, perhaps, dumped her, sending her into this fit of final despair.

If this sort of tragedy was not unknown to Washington, neither was it unique to that city.

For this once, he had invited her to drive directly to him; Edward was off tonight, he told her, so there would be no chauffeured limo ride from the Watergate.

But Edward was not off. Edward—the towering discrete manservant with the faintly British accent and long, blankly cruel face, a combination driver/cook/

valet highly recommended to him by a senator friend of his from Massachusetts—was waiting in the wings for Miss Petersen's cocktail to kick in, after which he carried her to the garage where the Jag waited.

The limo, parked on the street for this once, was to follow Rawson and his deceased passenger to this prearranged spot, and Edward was overdue. Just by two minutes, but that was not typical for Edward, and it unnerved Rawson, who was not thrilled to be standing on the roadside near a sports car with his own murdered mistress in it.

But then the limo rolled into view, kicking up some gravel dust, and soon Edward—uniformed, formal, so elegant and proper—stepped out, opened the back door of the black Lincoln Continental, and Rawson crawled into the secure, leather-smelling womb of it. Edward even had a drink waiting on the extended bar tray—a Dewars on ice.

"Unexpected traffic, sir," Edward said, as he took off.

"Thank you, Edward," Rawson said. "I'd like some privacy if you don't mind."

"Not at all, sir," the driver said, and closed the compartment off.

Rawson gulped greedily at the drink; he could not keep from looking back out the smoky glass window at the receding sight of the red Jag and the slumped blonde figure behind its wheel. When it was but a small red drop of blood on the moon-washed country landscape behind them, the limo took a hill, and the girl and the car were gone.

The following December, on a very cold lightly snowy night in Washington, D.C., against the advice of Edward (whose salary had been doubled after the "incident"), United States Senator Jim Rawson found himself, once again, drawn to the topless bar where he had met Vicki Petersen.

The Gentleman's Club, on M Street N.W., had been remodeled into a glittering chrome and mirrored wonderland, in the upscale fashion that was the current trend. Three stages, connected by runways, were being stalked by a trio of bare, bosomy beauties under disco-style flashing lights.

Rawson found a table against a mirrored wall and sat alone, away from the stages; he neither wanted to be noticed, nor to participate in the vulgar ritual of stuffing bills into dancer's G-strings. But watching these women was a hypnotic drug to him. He couldn't help himself. . . .

He was working on his second Dewar's—he'd been drinking too much lately, and he knew it, but that was another compulsion he couldn't control of late—when he noticed the girl on the center stage.

But for her black hair—a long flowing mane trailing clear down to the dimples of her perfect behind—she could have been damn near Vicki's twin: a heartbreakingly cute, pug-nosed thing with full high breasts and endless legs. She was graceful like Vicki, too, and sensual, swaying with the music.

His eyes were tearing up; it was smoky in there.

He called a waitress over—the shapely blonde

wore a tuxedo-like outfit, except her legs were exposed in fishnet hose. They had to shout at each other
to communicate; some mindless Madonna song was
blasting, the beat a pulsing thing.

"Please ask that dark-haired dancer to have a drink
with me," he yelled. He gave her two twenties and
told her to keep one for herself.

"Why, thank you, sir!" she hollered with wide-
eyed appreciation.

Half an hour later, the young woman approached
his table; she seemed to float to him, like an appari-
tion of Vicki— albeit a dark-haired one. That hair
was piled up high now, an ebony tower, and she was
in a low-cut black gown, breasts pushed up by an
engineering wonder of a brassiere, one long supple
leg exposed by a slit up the side to her hip.

She extended a black-gloved hand. "Charmed,
Senator."

That threw him. He had hoped not to be recognized. But such was the price of fame.

"What's your name, dear?" he asked, rising, getting her chair.

"Brandi," she said. "I'm a big admirer of yours,
Senator."

Her voice was surprisingly cultured; it was also a
low, cat-like purr. Vicki had never seemed cat-like
to him, but this woman—who otherwise resembled
Vicki so—was truly feline. Part of it was the black
hair. Part of it was an almost oriental slant to the eyes,
which wasn't like Vicki at all, though the China-blue

color of them was.

His tongue felt thick as he responded. "Admirer of mine?"

"Women's rights issues are important to me. So are issues of censorship. Any thinking person in my profession wants to see the arts protected."

"A wise point of view. You, uh . . . you're a very graceful dancer, Brandi."

"Thank you. I apologize for the surroundings."

"Why . . . this is downright elegant, here."

She averted his gaze. "I feel ashamed, working in a 'titty bar.' Glitz or not, that's what this is."

"I suppose. But I'm the one who should feel ashamed . . . I'm a patron, after all."

"A patron of the arts," she said, and her smile was white and dazzling, her lips transfusion-red. "I *am* a dancer, and an actress. I'm only here because the money is good, and other opportunities just aren't there, right now."

"Times are difficult. Show business is a . . . challenging profession, in the best of times. Of course, I do have certain connections ..."

She brushed his open palm with fingertips; even with the gloves on, her touch seemed warm. "Oh—I wish I knew you better, Senator. I could use a well-connected friend."

"Brandi, I . . . have to be honest with you. I'm a married man."

"I know. I've read about you. I know about your . . . tragedy."

He swallowed. "Pardon?"

Her expression seemed genuinely compassionate. "Your wife's illness. You have to stand beside her. Do the right thing by her. But still and all ... a man needs companionship."

Her hand was on his thigh, under the table.

"And a real man," she said, "needs even more."

He walked with her through the underground passageway, saying, "If you come again, my dear, you'll have to allow Edward—my chauffeur—to pick you up and bring you here. I can't risk being seen . . ."

"I understand. Your re-election campaign."

He nodded. "Next year's going to be a busy time for me."

"Even so, you'll need to relax, now and then."

Her arm was in his; she was snuggling against him.

In his study, on the leather sofa, basking in the glow and warmth of the fireplace, over which a serene Bingham landscape hung, they lay locked in an embrace. His hand was on her breast and her lips were nuzzling his neck.

"Senator," she said. She seemed to be fighting her own urges. "Please . . ."

He drew away. "Is something wrong?"

She sat up and he settled in beside her, looking at her curiously. "Senator, I... I had hoped we could get to know each other."

"Well, I thought that was what we were doing."

She smiled; leaned in and kissed him, quickly. "You're a rogue."

It seemed an odd, almost archaic choice of words to him, even if apt.

"What did you have in mind, Brandi?"

"First of all, my real name is Sheila. Sheila Douglas." She presented her hand, in mock formal fashion, and he grinned, shook his head, then the hand.

"Hello, Sheila. You're not a reporter are you?"

"No! No. Brandi's just my stage name. I'm a dancer at Gentleman's Club, with pretensions toward a show business career. Just as you thought. But I truly do want a friendship with you . . . well—I want more than a friendship. I want a relationship."

"I see."

"I felt . . . some chemistry between us, at the club. In the limo. In that passageway downstairs. Didn't you?"

"Frankly," he admitted, "yes."

"I know I can't ever be your wife. But I would like to be your . . . woman. The only woman in your life."

"Well, Brandi . . . Sheila ..."

"Maybe you don't want to make that commitment. I understand. But just because I have the body of a whore doesn't mean I am one. After all, topless clubs are popular because sex isn't safe, anymore."

"Interesting piece of sociology."

"Thank you. What I'm saying is ... if you're interested in me, as a person, as a friend, as a potential long-term relationship ... a loving one, I think, possibly ... I have to demand a ... a period of courtship."

He laughed a little. "You're from the Midwest,

aren't you?"

"Minnesota. Brainerd. We're both a couple of farmers, Jim. You mind if I call you 'Jim'?"

"Please. Have you had dinner?"

"No."

"Edward grills a mean steak."

"I'm a vegetarian."

"Well, he tosses a hell of a salad, too. Shall I put that in motion?"

She smiled, nodded; touched his knee.

They ate in the small, dark-wood-dominated dining room, under the miniature but intricate crystal chandelier. There was an elegance to it, and the mood of a . . . date. Much as he might want to get laid, he had to admit he liked the romance of this.

They retired to the study where the fire was dwindling; they sat and kissed and nuzzled. Tricky Dick came bouncing in and jumped up, straddling them.

She squealed, but it was a squeal of delight.

"What a beautiful big tomcat! Mixed breed?"

Rawson scratched Dick's ears. "Yes. I took him in off the street."

The cat was standing on her lap, now, staring right at her, as if searching out a secret.

Sheila smiled at him. "We're one of a kind, Mr. Kitty, you and me. Strays this good Samaritan here brought in off the street."

Then Tricky Dick curled up on her lap and she stroked him; he purred orgasmically.

"He's doing better than I am," Rawson said wryly.

"He likes me. Cats aren't always this affectionate."

"Dick's pretty easy-going, for a cat, but he seldom takes to strangers like this. I knew someone once who ..."

He stopped short.

"What is it?" she asked.

He rose; went to the liquor cart and poured himself a tumbler of Dewar's. "Nothing," he said.

Tricky Dick had taken to Vicki just like that. Just that way. . . .

"Where's his collar?" she asked.

He sat back down beside her. "He doesn't have one. He's a fat lazy old boy who never leaves the house. His litterbox is as close to the great-out-of-doors as he gets."

"Poor, poor kitty," she said, petting him. "How can you be so cruel, Senator? I'm going to buy you a collar," she said to the cat. "You mind if I do that, Jim? Buy your kitty cat a collar?"

"Not at all—if you can get him to wear the damn thing." She was scratching the cat's neck; it purred rapturously. "I think he'll love the attention," she said. "He's a male,

after all. Males do love attention. ..."

"Sir," Edward said, later, "do you know where Miss Douglas lives?"

"No," Rawson admitted. He was still in the study, seated on the couch, Tricky Dick curled up next to him, now; another tumbler of Dewar's in hand.

"The Watergate."

Rawson shrugged. Sipped. "A lot of people live at

the Watergate."

"Miss Petersen once lived at the Watergate, sir."

"Your point being?"

"We know nothing about this young lady. Perhaps you should hire an investigator to look into her background."

"If anything serious begins to develop, I will. Is that all, Edward?"

"Yes, sir. Sir?"

"What is it, Edward?"

"About my raise ..."

"You've had a raise."

"I'd like another, sir."

"I don't want to discuss this now, Edward."

"Fine, sir. But, sir?"

"*Yes,* Edward?"

"We *will* be discussing it, sir."

Three nights later, Sheila Douglas—wearing a baby-blue sweater and black ski pants and heels—was again a guest in Rawson's P Street townhouse. Edward prepared a seafood fettuccine (her vegetarianism, it seemed, pertained only to red meat) and the conversation was friendly. He prodded her about her show business aspirations, and she talked about actresses she admired—Faye Dunaway was her favorite, but she also liked Debra Winger. Chit chat.

In the study, he sat on the couch, patted the spot next to him and she took it. She gave him a long, lingering kiss. Her tongue flicked at his teeth.

"Where's Tricky Dick?" she asked.

"My cat?"

"What other Tricky Dick do you have? Or should I ask?"

He grinned, laughed, said, "You want to make me blush, young lady?" Then he whistled for the cat. When Dick wasn't curled up in the study, on the couch by his master, he slept in a little bed in a corner of the kitchen.

"He doesn't always come," Rawson said. "He *is* a cat, you know."

She called out. "Dick! Oh, Dick!"

And, soon, the cat came ambling in. The damn thing almost seemed to smile at her. It hopped up on her lap and began rubbing its head against her fuzzy sweater.

"He always gets a better shake out of you than me," Rawson said with a grin.

Her little purse was nearby on an end table. She reached for it and withdrew a sack with a pet-shop name on it; she took from the sack a heavy yellowish leather strap decorated with a few varicolored jewels.

"I hope Dick doesn't find the glitz effeminate," she said. "But it caught my eye at the pet store."

Rawson folded his arms. "Let's see if he stands still for *this* ..."

The cat seemed to crane its neck yearningly as she fitted the collar about his neck, no protests. In fact, it was clear he liked the goddamn thing!

"You're a wonder, Sheila. But now I have something for you."

He rose and went to a drawer in the mahogany tambour secretary against the wall. He removed the simple strand of glittering diamonds and held it out gently as he walked over to her.

"It's not a collar, exactly," he said. "In fact, it's just a bracelet."

"Oh, Jim! It's lovely! A tennis bracelet. . . oh, I've always wanted one ..."

She affixed it to her wrist and then held out her slender, red-nailed hand and gazed at the sparkling stones appreciatively. "Oh, Jim. How can I ever thank you?"

He sat down, slipped his arm around her. "There are . . . traditional ways I could think of."

She kissed him. The sound of the purring cat, as she stroked it, provided distracting background music.

"I think I could love you, Sheila."

"I feel that way about you, Jim. And I will thank you for this lovely gift. I want you to know I'll thank you the right way for it, too. But ..."

"Still too soon? I can wait. I'm a patient man."

She smirked and shook her head. "It's not that. It's .. . you know. The wrong time of the month for me. I'm sorry."

"Don't apologize for biology. That's what this is all about anyway, isn't it? Biology."

"Partly," she admitted. She stroked his face with one hand, her other hand petting the purring cat.

A week later, Rawson was getting worried about Sheila. He had called her at the Gentleman's Club and she'd been warm, friendly, but hadn't made another date with him.

"Please understand," she said. "I . . . this is embarrassing."

"What?"

"I have really long, hard periods, okay? Cramps you wouldn't believe. And cramps or not, right now I have to keep this lousy dancing up, to keep the rent paid."

"Well, I can handle that. Quit! I'll take care of you."

"Jim . . . you're wonderful. But it *is* too soon to talk that way. Next week. I promise."

That had been almost a week ago; several similar but briefer conversations had followed. Last night, out of desperation, he had gone to the club, looking for her; he was told she no longer worked there. He had even risked going to the Watergate, personally, to her apartment, where his knocking at her door went unanswered.

Now, early the following morning, he sat in his silk robe, brooding in his study, staring at the unlighted fireplace, scratching Tricky Dick around his collar.

"Sir . . ."

"Edward! I didn't hear you. Where the hell's my breakfast, man?"

"It'll have to wait, sir."

"Why in hell?"

"You should see the morning papers, sir. It's . . . not good, sir."

"What are you talking about?"

Edward, looking solemn, and dressed in a dark suit with dark tie that represented his street clothes, handed him the *Washington Post.*

The headline shouted RAWSON SUSPECT IN MURDER INVESTIGATION, and above it a smaller heading said: POLICE SOURCES SAY. Just glancing, he took in his own picture, and another of Vicki, under which were the words SUICIDE OR MURDER?

Edward spoke in a whisper: "She is the girl's sister."

"What ..."

"Sheila Douglas."

"What the hell are you saying, Edward?" Rawson was transfixed by this front page from Hell.

"Sheila Douglas," Edward said slowly, as if speaking to a child, his barely audible voice nonetheless like a scream in Rawson's brain, "is Vicki Petersen's sister."

"Edward . . . ?"

"She took a job where her sister had danced, hoping you would return to the scene of the crime. She had reason to believe you would. Apparently, the late Vicki had told her all about you."

"Oh my God."

"When you take time to read that article, you'll discover that Miss Douglas . . . actually, Miss Petersen, Sheila Petersen . . . has given the authorities tapes of conversations between myself. . . your 'major domo' . . . and you, sir."

"Oh. Oh God. Just two nights ago ... we negotiated

your latest raise . . ."

Edward continued in a barely audible, increasingly harsh whisper. "And we mentioned Miss Petersen's murder, the other Miss Petersen that is, as the motivation behind that salary increase. Yes, sir. The little bitch has had this town-house bugged."

"That's impossible! And this story is impossible. If this had been brewing, my phone would have rung off the hook last night with police and reporters ..."

"Have you seen your answering machine, sir? The little red light is blinking furiously."

Rawson's hand came to his face. "Oh my God, Edward! Where does that leave us?"

"I had hoped you might have some thoughts on that subject." Edward sighed. "But since you don't ..."

Edward's hand came out from behind his back and swung the wrench.

Rawson's surprised expression, below his caved-in skull, remained frozen as he toppled off the couch onto the parquet floor, where blood began to spill, then pool, glisteningly.

Tricky Dick, the cat, startled, leapt from the couch, looking for safe haven. Edward didn't consider the cat worthy of notice as he wiped the bloody wrench clean of his prints, thinking, *For what good it will do me,* and made his escape out the underground passageway.

His escape from the house, that is.

In the alley, the police were waiting. Edward sighed, put up his hands; in the police car, nearby, sitting on the rider's side in front, was Sheila Petersen.

She was smiling like the cat that ate the canary.

As for Tricky Dick, he was asleep in his bed in the corner of the kitchen. The only thing the tiny transmitter in his collar was picking up now was the deep, purring-like sound of the tom's breathing.

World's Greatest Mother

Mark Twain once came to town. He wrote about seeing the most magnificent sunsets here. Nestled serenely on the Mississippi River, our little city offers its citizens good quality life.

But all life ends, eventually. Sometimes abruptly.

My name is Joan Munday. My partner is Frank Lausen. We make up one-third of the six man—actually, five man, one woman—detective unit of the Port City Police Department.

It was Saturday, June 18, a day so perfect I could have killed to be out with Dan and the kids on the river: but instead, Frank and I were called to a new housing addition on the north side of town.

The homes in Mark Twain Meadows were expensive—by small town standards, anyway—with manicured lawns and well-tended flower gardens. The streets had quaint names— Samuel Clemens Road, Tom Sawyer Drive and Huckleberry Finn Lane.

We pulled up in front of 714 Pollyanna Place, and got out.

Walter, our crime lab technician, met us at the door. He was pushing fifty, balding, and looking tired.

"This way," he said, turning.

We followed.

The living room was tastefully decorated—perhaps too tastefully; it could have been the showroom of a pricey furniture store: couch and chairs matching in fabric, pictures and knick-knacks coordinating in color, all working together in harmony to produce somebody's idea of wonderful. Not mine. I couldn't imagine anyone "living" in this living room.

And there was one person who obviously agreed with me.

He was stretched out on the floor, on his face, in front of the fireplace, like a big bear rug. About six feet, two hundred pounds, he wore black cowboy boots, blue jeans and a torn white T-shirt. His hair was blonde—except on the left side of his head, where it was now a blackening red.

Walter broke the silence. "A single blow to the head. His name is Travis ..."

"I know who he is," I cut in.

Every town has a bully. Travis Wykert was ours. As far back as junior high, his penchant for pounding those smaller than him had got him in trouble with the law. As an adult, he'd been brought up several times on assault charges, but no one would testify.

"That the weapon?" asked Frank. He was a sandy-haired, husky man in his late twenties—ten years younger than me. He gestured toward the couch, where a trophy lay encased in a clear plastic bag.

Walter nodded. "Wiped clean."

"Went there," Frank said, pointing to the mantle above the fireplace. "See the spot in the dust?"

I looked, and caught my reflection in the large mirror over the fireplace; should have spent a little more time on my hair this morning.

I crossed over and picked up the bagged trophy, a heavy bronze statue of a woman holding a baby. A plaque on its base read *World's Greatest Mother.*

"Where's the owner?" I asked Walter.

"In the kitchen," he said, "down the hall."

The kitchen, in the back of the house, was a bright, spacious room, so clean the cabinets gleamed. But like the living room, it too didn't look lived in. There was nothing on the counters, not even a toaster. Lace curtains framed the windows, while flocks of country geese roamed the walls.

At a round, oak table sat three women. The one on the left, smoking a cigarette, was middle-aged. She wore dark slacks and a black turtleneck top. Her brown hair, streaked with gray, was short, mannish. She wore no make-up.

The woman in the middle, in a white skirt and a blouse with kittens on it, was also middle-aged. Her hair was dark blonde, shoulder-length; her face was obscured, buried in her hands as she sobbed.

The one on the right was young and slender, with long, ice-blonde hair. She wore jeans and a sweatshirt with a Port City Community College logo on it. The girl sat motionless, in apparent shock, staring, her face a mask.

A uniformed cop, who was first at the scene, stood behind them taking notes on a pad.

"This is Louise Harris," he said, pointing to the woman in the middle. "She owns the house. And this is her daughter, Laura." He gestured to the young girl. Then he nodded to the woman on the left. "That's Pamela Schultz. She's renting a room."

I approached them. "Who wants to tell me about it?" I asked.

Pamela Schultz threw her head back and blew out smoke, then stubbed her cigarette out in an ashtray. "He was hurting Laura so I hit him," she said, matter-of-factly, like she was giving me the weather report.

Louise Harris looked up from her hands. Her eyes were red, swollen, her face puffy. "Don't try to protect me, Pam," she said, "*I* did it."

Now the younger woman, Laura, turned her face toward me, slowly, robot-like. "They're both lying," she said softly, and then announced, as if ending a game of *Clue.* "I killed Travis Wykert in the living room with the trophy."

It was 4:35 in the afternoon when we got back to the Public Safety Building—a big, modern, red-brick affair we shared with the Fire Department.

We were faced with a unique problem: usually it was hard enough getting *one* confession; now we had three.

The women had each been Mirandized; all three declined an attorney.

I waited with Frank in the interrogation room.

"Because the suspects are female," I said to him, "we might do better if I take the lead. But jump in when you want to."

He nodded.

"But no good cop, bad cop crap," I warned.

"Got ya."

The interrogation room door opened and Pamela Schultz was brought in. I nodded toward a chair. She sat, sullenly, legs crossed, one hand resting casually on the table.

"I called your probation officer in Colorado," I said. "She said she couldn't understand why you left friends and a good-paying job to come here."

"I had permission," the woman shrugged. "Maybe I just wanted to do something different."

"Like work at McDonald's?"

She looked away.

"What's your relationship with Louise Harris?" Frank asked.

She looked over at him. "I'm renting a room from her," she said.

Frank smirked.

Pamela's eyes narrowed. "We're not *lovers,* if

that's what you're getting at . . . God, you *men* are all alike."

Then she looked at me. "And *you're* just as bad ... I can tell what you're thinking."

No, she couldn't—but I let it go.

"How well did you know Travis Wykert?" I asked.

"I've never met him before today," she said. Then she leaned forward, spreading the fingers of the hand that lay on the table. "Look—I've already given you people a confession. What more do you want? That creep was beating on Laura so I stopped him. If you ask me, I did the world a favor."

I leaned in. "Then why are *both* Louise Harris and her daughter taking credit for your good deed?"

"How the hell should I know!" she said. "I mean, do you *really* think either of them could have done it? Louise is afraid of her own shadow, and Laura was obviously under the spell of that sadistic bastard."

"So *you* stepped in," Frank said.

"I've done it before."

I looked at Frank; he raised his eyebrows.

I walked around the table and stood next to Pamela Schultz, placing a hand on the back of her chair. "And paid twenty long years for it," I said, putting compassion into my voice. "But it doesn't hardly seem right," I continued, "considering how that man abused you."

Her body stiffened.

"Back then," I said, moving closer, "rights for abused women weren't in fashion." I whispered in her ear, "Today you would have *walked.*"

A look of agony passed over her face, then sudden rage.

"I *told* you I killed the bastard," she snapped back. "Now quit wasting my damn time!"

"If you did kill him," I said, "you'll be doing plenty."

"Plenty of what?" she smirked.

"Time."

*****

Louise Harris sat fidgeting, a bundle of twitches and tics. I couldn't make up my mind whether to come on strong and watch her dissolve into a puddle of protoplasm, or take a more humane approach.

I chose the latter.

"Just relax," I said to her, reassuringly. "That's right, take some deep breaths. Now, I want to know exactly what happened this morning."

She sighed. "It was about eleven," she said, her voice quavering. "Pam—she's renting a room from me—and I were in the kitchen having coffee when I heard the front door bang open. Somehow, instinctively, I knew it was him, and I was frightened for Laura ..."

"Why?"

"He's hit her before. A few weeks ago she came home with a black eye. Said she'd run into something. But I knew who did it. I told her I was going to call the police . . . but she said she wouldn't cooperate."

Louise Harris looked at me with sad, swollen eyes.

"Do you know what it's like to have to sit by and watch your child throw her life away?" she asked. "Ever since her father walked out on us five years ago, it's like she wants *every* man in her life to treat her badly."

Mrs. Harris buried her head in her hands and sobbed.

I took some Kleenex from a box on the table and handed it to her. She wiped her eyes and blew her nose.

I waited for her to compose herself.

"Getting back to this morning," I said, "where was Laura when Travis Wykert entered the house?"

"Laura was in the living room, reading," Louise said. "By the time I ran out of the kitchen, that man had her cornered in front of the fireplace. He was shouting at her, slapping her."

"What was he shouting?" Frank asked.

Louise looked at Frank, then turned her head, avoiding his gaze. "I . . . don't remember," she said haltingly. "Obscenities. Things ..."

"Then what?" I asked.

"Pamela—she was standing next to me—tried to pull him off Laura, but he threw Pam onto the davenport. That's when I picked up the trophy and ..."

She lowered her head, crying softly into the tissue.

"Come now, Mrs. Harris," I scoffed gently, "you don't have the stomach to commit murder, now, do you? Stop covering up for Pamela Schultz. The most she'd get is manslaughter."

Louise Harris looked up angrily. "May I ask you something?"

I nodded.

"Do you have any children?"

I nodded again.

"Then you can understand how a parent feels when their child is in danger . . . you would give your life for that child, you would do anything . . . even kill."

The woman was right.

"And I *hated* that man!" Louise Harris said viciously. "I wanted him out of Laura's life!"

I looked down at her. "I'm afraid you've got that wrong, Mrs. Harris."

"How's that?"

"He isn't out of her life yet."

"I'd been seeing Travis for about six months," said Laura. She seemed composed, but her eyes were haunted. "Could I please have a glass of water?"

I looked at Frank, who left the room.

"I know what people thought of him," Laura said, "but I saw something different: a frightened, abused little boy. His father beat him. I guess I thought I could help him—which was a laugh, considering what my *own* father did to me ..."

Frank returned with the glass of water and set it on the table in front of Laura, who took a drink.

I waited.

"A while back," she continued, "I came home with a black eye. Travis and I had an argument." She paused. "Well, actually, I won't lie . . . he hit me for no good reason. My m-mother was furious. She wanted to press charges against Travis, but I told her I loved him and I wouldn't cooperate."

Laura took another sip of water.

"Shortly after that, she rented a room out to that woman. At the time I couldn't understand why—we didn't *need* the money."

"Did you know the Schultz woman was convicted of murder?" I asked.

She shook her head, then she nodded, "Not at first. But I found out later."

"Your mother brought this woman in to kill Travis Wykert," I said flatly.

"No!" Laura said sharply, "That's not true!"

"Then what is?"

She took a deep breath and exhaled. "Pamela Schultz is my m-mother."

"What?" Frank and I said.

"My natural m-mother."

Frank and I exchanged wide-eyed glances.

"How did you find out?" I asked.

"I think I always suspected. But I knew for sure the moment I saw Pamela Schultz . . . and my own eyes looked back at me."

Laura told us that she had confronted her adoptive mother who said that she and Pam were best friends in high school. After graduation Pam got married and moved away. A year later when Pam came to visit Louise—who herself had gotten married—she had a new baby. But Pam didn't seem happy. Pam asked Louise to take care of the newborn while she visited another friend. It was a few days later that Louise heard Pam had killed her husband.

"So my m-mother . . . Louise Harris . . . kept me as her own," Laura said, "and never told me about any of it. . . until my *real* mother came around ..."

The room fell silent.

"Why did she come around?" I asked, finally.

"To try to talk some sense into me."

"About Travis abusing you?"

"Yes."

Frank asked, "Why was Travis so pissed off when he came to see you this morning?"

Laura winced. "He wanted me to get an abortion. I told him I wouldn't."

"Did your mother know you were pregnant?" I asked.

"Which one?"

Frank rolled his eyes.

"Either," I said.

"Well, they *both* knew after he started yelling about it."

"Then what happened?" I asked.

"When Travis hit me, Pamela attacked him. But he threw her off. Then Travis looked back at me with such hatred that I was really frightened ... I was scared for me, and the baby! I grabbed the nearest thing I could get my hands on, a trophy I had given my m-mother ..."

Laura stared at her hands. "Funny," she said, "a decision you make in a split second can change the rest of your life . . . or somebody else's . . ."She looked up at me with eyes that pierced me.

"Don't you see?" she said, pleadingly, "I had no choice. I *couldn't* get an abortion."

She shook her head. "No . . . there was just no way I was going to do that. After all . . . that would be murder."

It was 8:45 that evening when I stood with Frank on the steps of the Public Safety Building, watching the three women get into the backseat of a squad car.

We let them go. For now.

"I have a feeling," I said slowly, "that we may never solve this one. Hell. Maybe I should have been tougher on 'em."

The car door slammed shut.

"Know what I think?" Frank said.

"What?"

"I think that each of those women *thinks* that *she* really did it . . ."

The car pulled away from the curb.

"... that for one moment, in front of the fireplace, the urge to kill Travis Wykert entered all of their minds . . . and then it didn't matter whose hand actually held the trophy."

I looked at Frank. "But if you had to pick one, who would it be?"

He looked at me, shrugged. "Who cares who killed Travis Wykert?"

We watched the squad car, until it disappeared into one of those magnificent sunsets Mark Twain wrote about.

"Not me," I said.

Then we went back into the station.

A Cruise to Forget

Before he signed on as medical officer aboard the Carnival Fun Ship *Fantasy,* Dr. Tom Swayze had interned at Cook County Hospital. At first, the excitement of working in the notorious Chicago emergency room exhilarated him, made him feel indispensable and important; but, in time, the incessant array of blood and pain, torn tissue and red tape, began to chip away at him, and one day the thirty-one-year-old bachelor woke up feeling that if he didn't get out of that Dante's Inferno of an E.R. soon, he would be the next patient admitted, strapped to a gurney and shuttled off to the nearest psychiatric unit.

When a former colleague approached him to work for the Carnival line, Tom eagerly "jumped ship" and turned in his hospital resignation. The idea of sun and snorkeling and shipboard romances was irresistibly seductive—fun, even glamorous activities he'd never had time for in his current life.

But after four years of sun and snorkeling and shipboard romances, Dr. Tom Swayze—his hair sun-lightened to the color of a sandy tropical beach, his boyish, round-as-a-coconut face handsomely tanned—woke up one day feeling that if he didn't get off this ship soon, they'd be wheeling him down the gangway, strapped to a gurney and shuttled off to the nearest psychiatric unit.

Shipboard life, he found, was incredibly boring, and this latest cruise was no exception. The *Fantasy* was about to leave Port Canaveral, Florida, for a four-day trip to Nassau, and out of two thousand passengers only three had bothered to look him up in his office adjacent the infirmary on the Main Deck. Two were a husband and wife, Anthony and Margaret Vane, who the doctor found seated in his outer office after coming back from the pharmacy.

The husband was perhaps in his early fifties, suavely handsome, already deeply tanned, with dark, slicked-back hair in the time-honored Valentino fashion, and dark, deep-set eyes hooded with apparent concern. He was wearing tailored tan linen slacks and a silk cream-colored shirt, open at the neck, his black chest hair curling out; his left hand sported an expensive gold watch and a gold ring with a diamond that was no larger than the knuckle it rode.

Seated next to the aptly named Mr. Vane, the wife was a bundle of twitches and tics. Perhaps fifteen or even twenty years older than her husband, she had been beautiful once, but her face had been ravaged by one too many lifts. She, too, was expensively dressed, wearing a white pants suit with gaudy silver rhinestones and too much jewelry.

"Margaret, I'm afraid, has misplaced her medication," Anthony Vane said, after introducing his wife and himself to the doctor. There was mild irritation in his tone, but Vane seemed, for the most, anxious, genuinely worried for his companion's welfare.

"I'm so sorry, dear," she said to him, her body moving in jerky, bird-like fashion. "I'm afraid I'm getting forgetful in my old age."

Vane slipped his hand in hers. "You? Never . . . But it *was* hectic at the hotel—we stayed overnight at Cape Canaveral, and I blame myself, really. When she's feeling good, my wife tends to put her medication out of her mind ..."

"That's understandable," the doctor said.

Vane smiled tenderly at his elderly bride. "I just don't want anything to spoil this trip for you, dear."

Her smile in response was more a twitch than a smile. "I'm sure we can remedy the situation," Swayze told them, in his practiced, calm tone. It was what he said to everyone who came to see him, to put them at ease. He gestured toward his inner office.

Once inside, with the couple seated in front of him, Swayze sat behind his desk as Vane handed the doctor a folded sheet of paper.

"It's a letter from our doctor," the man explained.

"Just in case something like this might happen. You can give him a call if you like."

Swayze read the note regarding the woman's medication, which was written on stationery from a Fifth Avenue doctor in New York. Fifth Avenue doctors didn't seem to have any better penmanship than anyone else in the medical fraternity

"This will be fine," Swayze told them. "I'll just make a photocopy and return it to you." He looked at the wife, fidgeting in her chair. "And I'll need to ask you a few questions ..." He consulted the letter again. "... uh, Margaret?"

Her reply was a mouse-like squeak: "Yes."

He gave her his best bland, meaningless physician's smile. "How long have you been taking this anti-depressant, Margaret?"

The woman peered sideways at her husband as if asking permission to answer. He nodded reassuringly.

"About a year now."

"And you feel it's helping your depression?"

Again she looked at her husband, who again nodded.

"I think it is," she said.

Swayze didn't. He thought this bundle of nerves needed something a whole lot stronger, and soon. But it wasn't his job aboard ship to fix a gaping wound, just slap a Band-Aid on it.

He wrote on his prescription pad. "This should be sufficient to carry you through the cruise . . . Then you'll need to see your own physician as soon as you get back, understand?"

The woman smiled, relieved. "I will, and thank you doctor."

"Don't hesitate to come see me again if you have any more trouble," he told them, as he told everyone when they left.

The *third* person who came to see him the morning the ship sailed for Nassau required a bit more of his time; but he didn't mind—he had plenty of it to spare. And besides, she was attractive, and (he soon discovered) single.

Wearing navy slacks and a red top decorated with little gold anchors, the thirty-something blonde with shoulder-length hair sat across from his desk, her poise undermined by hazel eyes that hinted that not all was well, and in fact carried a look of controlled hysteria.

"Thank you for your time, doctor," she said. Her voice was a melodic alto. "You're probably very busy."

Swayze half-smiled, saying, "Whatever your problem is. I'm sure we can remedy it," then wondered if he'd sounded too openly flirtatious.

She shifted in her seat. "I wish you could," she said sadly, "but I don't think you'll be able to ... I don't think anyone would be."

He frowned.

"My name is Jennifer Kafer," she explained. "I'm on the cruise with my mother, Cora Hazen, and I have reason to believe she's in the early stages of Alzheimer's."

Swayze leaned forward in his chair. "I am sorry," he said. "You haven't seen a doctor at home, then?"

"No, this is a problem that has accelerated rather rapidly, I'm afraid," Jennifer said, and went on to explain. "After my father died last year, I had Mother move in with me and my six-year old daughter, Lisa, who's staying with her father while Mother and I take this trip . . . We've been divorced for several years."

He managed not to smile at this good news, keeping a professionally concerned expression in place; and he *was* concerned, even if his musings about this pretty passenger were somewhat less than professional.

"Anyway," Jennifer Kafer continued, "Mother seems fine most of the time—I would have canceled the trip, if she weren't—but every now and then, more and more often, Mother just isn't herself. She's almost like a child. Last week, I came home and found her playing with my daughter's Barbie dolls . . . She looked at me like she didn't know who I was. But then, a few hours later, she was back to her old self again."

Swayze leaned on his elbows and made a tent with his hands. "Has your mother shown any violent tendencies?"

Jennifer shook her head. "No, she's always quite cheerful." She paused, then added, "I guess I should be thankful for that. My girlfriend, Susan, her mother has Alzheimer's . . . and Susan's mother has turned *very* mean. Last year, when Susan bought a new television, her mother smashed it with a baseball bat and cursed her for buying a TV that played commercials. Her mother became so abusive she finally had to be institutionalized."

Swayze sat back in his chair and heaved a sympathetic sigh. "It's quite typical, people suffering with Alzheimer's venting their anger and frustration on family members. But if your mother remains cheerful, and content, as the disease progresses, you will indeed be lucky ... at least as lucky as a caretaker of a loved one with Alzheimer's could ever hope to be."

Jennifer nodded in agreement, then dug into her purse. "I'd like to give you this picture of her," she said. "Even though I'll be with her every moment on the ship, well . . . Sometimes small children can wander away, if you know what I mean." She placed the photo on his desk. "It could be helpful in finding her."

Swayze looked at the photo. "Is this a recent photo?"

"Just a year ago, before any signs had become apparent."

Cora Hazen was a vibrant older woman with short red hair, a dazzling smile and intelligent bright eyes that in time, he knew, would be dimmed by the insidious disease, robbing the poor woman, and her family, of the last years of her life.

"I could arrange to sit at your table during meals," the doctor offered.

Jennifer's face lighted up like fireworks off the starboard bow. "Oh, that's very generous, doctor!"

And it was a generous offer, but then, the lovely woman seated in front of him would be enjoyable company, and he'd grown tired of eating at the staff table.

"That is," he said, "if you think my observations might help, or at least give you some peace of mind."

"Oh they would, and I hope I can find some way to repay you, doctor," she said, her expression radiant.

He said, "No thanks are necessary," thinking that he hoped she would find a way, adding, "And of course, don't hesitate to come see me again if you have any more trouble."

When the woman had gone, Dr. Swayze put the picture of Cora Hazen aside, filed away his thoughts for a promising shipboard romance, and settled back in his chair for yet another uneventful cruise.

The ship's enormous Celebration dining room, located in the middle of the Atlantic Deck, was decorated as if every night were a party: carpet like colorful confetti, tables aglow with candles, streamers hanging from the ceiling, and everyone dressed to the nines; the whole place looked like a big birthday cake with all its candles glowing, ready for a wish.

Anthony wished he was on the boat with one of his several current, younger love interests, and not his stupid older wife. But, then, the three women he was having affairs with did not have Margaret's money. Margaret had Margaret's money— and for him to have to access to that tidy fortune, he had to put up with having Margaret.

It was the first evening meal of the cruise, and they were dining near the center of the room at one of the round, white-linen-sheathed tables that seated eight. He didn't know the others at his table (nor did he want to); they were just strangers thrown uncomfortably together for a few days. But by the end of the cruise, Margaret would know all of them intimately and add the whole boring bunch to their Christmas card list.

He looked at his wife, chattering away giddily, endlessly, to anyone who would listen, about their quiet country life in South Hampton alternating with travel like this "scrumptious cruise." Social situations like this gave her a means of channeling her nervous energy. He concentrated on his Beef Wellington and did his best not to show how he felt, or what he was thinking.

Earlier, when he first arrived in the dining room, he'd spotted Dr. Swayze several tables away, seated between a shapely thirty-ish blonde and an older attractive redhead— the lucky bastard. Either woman would have suited Anthony just fine—they both looked like they had money—but if he had his choice he'd pick the redhead; it wasn't so much that he had a penchant for older woman as they seemed to have a penchant for him.

It never occurred to him that perhaps younger women saw through his dated technique. After being seated, however, Anthony never looked their way again, other than to make sure the doctor didn't notice him perfidiously keeping his wife's wine glass filled.

Alcohol, in combination with her medication, made Mrs. Vane grow quiet . . . and depressed.

Thinking back, Anthony wasn't exactly sure when he first decided to do away with Margaret. At some point, the scales had tipped: living with a neurotic woman, and having anything her money could buy, seemed far less attractive than just having anything her money could buy.

In the beginning, it was a daydream, a fantasy; but he had returned to the thought again and again, until it hardened into reality . . .

He had met Margaret just over ten years ago in Central Park, when he was in his early forties and insolvent, having run through the meager inheritance left him by his previous wife, who had been in her seventies and whose estate had largely gone to her grown children. Margaret was younger than the previous Mrs. Vane—she'd just turned sixty—and was the childless widow of a Manhattan real estate tycoon, who'd made his mint long before Donald Trump came on the scene.

At first, the future Mrs. Vane had been cautious about sharing her wealth with him, and even spoke of a prenuptial agreement; but soon Anthony's talk of love and trust, plus his considerable sexual prowess, convinced her that there was more to life than money.

"Is anything the matter, dear?" he asked his wife sweetly. "You seem so quiet."

Morosely, she shook her head.

Voices from the doctor's table drifted to him, and

Anthony caught snatches of conversation. It seemed the two women dining with the physician were mother and daughter—the mother widowed, the daughter divorced. He wondered idly if they might be interested in a threesome? *Ménage* with a mother and daughter was on the short list of sexual adventures life had as yet denied him.

But it was the mother's youthful voice and musical laughter that made the front of his black tux pants tingle. He wanted to look the redhead's way, to catch a glimpse of her enticing smile, but instead he adjusted his linen napkin in his lap and forced himself to carry on a conversation with the stodgy banker from Boston seated next to him.

After the main course plates had been cleared, Anthony leaned toward his wife and said, "You don't look at all well, my dear—you seem rather peaked. Why don't we go for a stroll on deck?"

She peered at him, blue eyes touched by a filigree of red. "I don't care to. Dessert is coming."

He gave her a little smile. "Just thought you might like to catch a little air, sweetheart."

The others at the table had stopped their conversation and were looking the couple's way; but Margaret didn't seem to notice.

Anthony leaned toward her and, giving her an affectionate peck on the cheek, asked, "Then you won't mind if I stretch my legs for a while?"

What to the other passengers might seem an innocent question to Margaret was a veiled threat. She knew, as well as her husband, that there were any number of lonely women on board the *Fantasy,* eager to meet a handsome stranger.

"I've changed my mind," she said abruptly, placing her napkin on the table. "I'll get some air with you."

Their fellow diners had noticed his wife's dramatic mood swing—from belle of the ball to sullen wallflower—and this suited Anthony's plans ideally.

As they exited the dining room, Anthony put a comforting arm around his wife, as if she were ailing. And when they passed the doctor's table, Anthony maintained his concerned expression, his eyes fixed only upon his dearly beloved.

On the Upper Deck, he opened the heavy wood door inset with oval cut-glass and the burst of weather from the outside was almost enough to make Margaret turn back; the wind was strong, the night black, and a slight drizzle spat insolently in their faces.

"My hair!" she wailed, both hands flying to the sides of her head. She had spent two hours in the ship's beauty shop that afternoon, a waste of time and money, in her husband's opinion; her looks were gone, like his patience with her.

He ignored her plea, ushering her out on the narrow platform and over to the steel rail. The deck was deserted; everyone else was still in the dining room, gorging themselves on pastries and pies, and even the non-gluttons had been warded off by the weather.

Mr. Vane had planned on taking Mrs. Vane in his arms and kissing her one last time—he really was a romantic, and once had felt something akin to love for her, when she was still attractive. One last kiss, remembering some of the good times . . . But since nothing came to mind, he gathered her in his arms, like a bride about to be ushered over the threshold, and—her eyes wide, her mouth open, as she tried desperately to make this a romantic gesture—he hurled her unceremoniously over the rail.

He was surprised at how light she'd seemed in his arms, and how quickly she disappeared into the ocean, the black, white-capped waves reaching upward as if to catch her, then pulling her down and under.

She'd been too surprised to scream; or had she simply accepted her fate, would rather be dead than unloved by him? Anthony would never know, and would also never ponder the answer again.

He lingered only a second or two before turning toward the outer deck door to leave. The door was being partially held open by someone.

Hell!

It was the red-haired woman, the attractive older widow, who had stepped out onto the deck—her daughter was nowhere to be seen. How long she'd been there, Anthony didn't know; but her expression of shock told him what she'd seen.

Everything.

He froze, horrified, not knowing what to do. And as voices trailed out to him from the open door, telling him others were on their way to the deck, he realized there wasn't time for the woman named Cora Hazen to join his wife under the choppy sea.

"I. . . I. . ." He could only stammer as he took a few tentative steps toward her, his suave facade dropping like pants whose suspenders had snapped.

Cora Hazen let go of the door and plastered herself against the wall of the deck.

"Please keep quiet," he said, gathering the shreds of his dignity about him. "I have money ... A great deal of money."

Her eyes seemed oddly blank, then came alive. "Money? Let me see!"

He quickly dug into his pants pocket and brought out a wad of cash that had been meant for the casino, later that night, and thrust it toward her.

"This is all I have on me . . . but I can get you more, much more ..."

Her eyes were as wide as Margaret's going over the side; but her face had taken on a child-like glee.

"I *like* money!" she said and snatched the cash from his hand.

He leaned an arm against the deck wall, pinning her there. "We're alike, you and I."

She gazed up at him girlishly. "You like money, too?"

What a tease!

"Oh yes," he said.

She was riffling through the money as if she were counting it, but not really keeping track, taunting him, the clever bitch.

So, the eyewitness to his crime was as greedy as he was, it seemed; this would be costly, but with

Margaret's fortune, he could control it. He could turn this around . . .

Then the deck door opened again, and the woman's daughter emerged. Cora quickly thrust the wad of bills behind her back.

"Mother," the pretty woman said anxiously, "I've been looking all over for you."

The daughter seemed oddly distraught.

"Dear," the mother said, "I've been talking to this nice gentleman." She leaned toward her daughter and added in a loud whisper, "He has a lot of m-o-n-e-y."

Damn her, needling him like this.

Fortunately, the daughter merely looked at him with embarrassment. "I'm sorry about this, Mr., uh . . . ?"

"Vane," he said with slight bow of his head. "Anthony Vane. It's so nice to meet you and your delightful mother."

"And you, too," the daughter said distractedly, then turned to the older woman. "Mother, it's time we get back to our stateroom."

"Yes, and I must try to find my wife," Anthony said. "I seem to have misplaced her." He laughed a little, sneaking a look at the mother. No reaction. Her lovely face remained cheerfully placid.

A cool customer, this one. Had he finally found the woman who was his equal?

"I hope you ladies have a pleasant evening," he said, bowing to the women. "Perhaps I'll be seeing you later."

The mother giggled. "If you're lucky."

Damn, if she wasn't a beguiling creature! He watched the pair go back inside, standing there with his heart pounding as if trying to burst from his rib cage. Funny—he'd been calm as he tossed Margaret overboard; only now was his pulse racing, fear and excitement coursing through him.

He leaned at the rail and breathed deeply of the cold night air. It was time to put the rest of his plan in motion—he would go to the casino for a few hours, then when he returned to his room and found his wife not there, he would search the ship (making sure his efforts were witnessed) and finally report that she was missing.

The cloak that was his suaveness gathered about him again, self-composed once more, he headed for Club 21 on the Promenade Deck, wondering what he should do about Cora—kill her, or make love to her.

Or both—in reverse order, of course. He wasn't sick, after all.

It was only when the dessert dishes were being cleared that Jennifer realized how long her mother had been away on her trip to the ladies' room, and began to panic. She had been engrossed in conversation with the doctor (Tom was single, she discovered, with a fascinating history as an E.R. doctor) when her mother had said she'd be right back.

But "right back" turned into fifteen minutes and Jennifer stopped listening to what the doctor was saying and began looking anxiously around the vast dining room.

"I'm sure she'll be along soon," Tom said, doing his best to put her at ease. "She seems fine tonight."

"It's so easy to forget," Jennifer said. "When she's behaving like herself, it's easy to treat her like the adult I knew."

"There's nothing to worry about—really."

Jennifer was shaking her head. "I shouldn't have let her go by herself. Even *I* can get lost on this big ship .. . And you just don't know how quickly she can *change.*" She stood, pushing back her chair.

"Why don't I go with you," the doctor offered, putting his napkin down. "We both can search."

Jennifer put a hand on his shoulder. "No. Let me look first, and if I can't find her, I'll come back and get you."

"You're sure? Because it's no trouble ..."

"I need to learn to handle situations like this," she told him, firmly but not unkindly, "myself."

Jennifer first checked the restrooms just outside the dining room near the elevators, then moved on to the Pavilion with its smaller restrooms, and finally descended the grand staircase in the center of the ship to the lower floor. As she hurried along she was reminded of the time she'd lost her own daughter in a big department store, and all kinds of terrible images had rampaged through her mind, until the child was at last found in the toy department, playing happily away with Barbie dolls.

Perhaps the Galleria Shops had caught her mother's attention; they were located back on the same deck as the dining room. She was taking a shortcut past the galley when she spotted her mother's red hair through the oval window of a deck door; her mother was standing on the windy deck, talking to a handsome middle-aged man.

When Jennifer went through the door into the cold, spitting sea air, she knew in an instant that her mother was not herself; she could tell by the animated way her mother was talking to the man, who, upon closer look, had the slick, archaic look of a Noel Coward-era gigolo. She remembered noticing him a few tables away, with a dejected-looking older woman seated at his side.

Jennifer got her mother away from the man as gracefully as she could—he seemed to be misinterpreting her infantile behavior as coquettish, thankfully—and, back in their stateroom, called and left word for the doctor that she had found her mother and that they were in for the night.

As Jennifer undressed, she wondered if the two of them were going to survive the trip; in a very short time her mother had gotten so much worse.

Their stateroom (so-called), on the Empress Deck, had two twin beds and an ocean view. It was a little cramped, but nice enough, the decor a soothing mauve and turquoise, with a TV high in one corner, a writing table with fresh flowers against one wall, and a lovely pastel picture of a tropical beach on another.

"I think we should get some sleep," Jennifer said to her mother. "It's been a very long day."

"But I'm not sleepy yet," her mother responded. She was sitting on one of the beds, bouncing ever so slightly.

"We're going to have an even longer, busier day tomorrow, Mother. We'll be docking in Nassau in the morning."

Her mother wrinkled her nose, as if smelling something icky.

"Why don't you get into your new nightgown," Jennifer cajoled. "I've put your things in the closet."

Her mother got up from the bed and went to the closet, but instead of retrieving her nightgown, she brought out a small pink suitcase, which she took back to the bed and opened. Jennifer sighed. "Mother, please don't get into that. It's late."

Her mother ignored her plea, rifling through the pink child-size suitcase—which had once belonged to Jennifer's daughter—filled with old and new Barbie dolls, accessories and tiny clothes.

Jennifer stared at her mother, who in her heyday had been one of the movers and shakers of the fashion world, designing and launching her own work-out clothes, long before any other designer had. Now she was stripped of any remaining talent, still somehow connected to fashion in the withering recesses of her mind, reduced now to playing with doll clothes, drawn to them, perhaps not even knowing why.

Mother looked up at daughter anxiously. "Where's Nibbles? I can't find Nibbles."

"We talked about that before we left, Mother,"

Jennifer said slowly, trying to stay calm but feeling exasperation begin to overwhelm her. "I told you we couldn't bring everything. Don't you *remember?*"

But, then, that was the whole problem, wasn't it?

"But I need Nibbles! You know Barbie will want to ride her horsey." She held up one of the dolls; its blonde hair was a mess, giving it a crazed look.

Jennifer closed her eyes, gathering all the strength she could. Then she went over and sat on her mother's bed and slipped an arm gently around the woman's shoulders.

"Look, Mom," she said tactfully, "you be a good girl and get to bed, and tomorrow we'll find another horsey in Nassau." It was a fib, of course, or close to one: Jennifer doubted any store on the island carried Barbie toys.

"But what if they don't *have* it? What then?" her mother sniffed, holding back tears.

"Then we'll buy something else, just as nice."

"Nicer!"

"Nicer."

"Like My Very Own Vanity for fifty-nine dollars and ninety-five cents? Or the Cruisin' Car convertible for thirty-four dollars and ninety-five cents?"

"That's right. One of those."

Her mother shifted on the bed, barely able to contain her enthusiasm. "Or the Malibu Beach House for ninety-nine dollars and ninety-five cents?"

"We'll see."

"I have my very own money, you know," her mother said, with a smile that was lovely if you didn't study it.

"Yes. Yes." Before the trip Jennifer had given her mother twenty dollars to carry; she didn't trust her with anything more. "But you have to get to bed, first."

"Goody goody goody! G'night . . . what's your name again, dear?"

"Jennifer, Mother. It's Jennifer."

"You're my daughter." Her mother seemed proud of this observation.

"Yes. Yes, I am."

Five minutes later, with the lights out and the ship rolling gently over and through the waves, steaming its way to Nassau, Jennifer lay in her bed staring up at the cabin ceiling.

How could her mother remember every single Barbie toy and exactly what it cost and *not* remember her own daughter's name? Such was the way of this maniacal disease.

Maybe someday, she thought, I'll laugh at the absurdity of it all.

But not tonight.

Jennifer waited until she heard her mother softly snoring before turning her head into the pillow and sobbing.

*****

It was a very distraught Anthony Vane who banged on Dr. Swayze's cabin door, well after four in the morning, waking him from a sound sleep.

"I just don't understand it," Anthony said, tightening his forehead as if in concern, working exasperation into his voice, words tumbling out. "I don't know where my wife could be. I took her back to our stateroom after dinner, then went off to the casino and stayed till closing."

The casino closed at three a.m.

"And when I returned shortly thereafter," Anthony continued, "she wasn't there."

"Now, just take it easy, Mr. Vane." The doctor put his hand on Anthony's shoulder. "Most likely you're just missing each other—she probably went to the casino to look for you, and—"

"No! No, I went back and checked, I've been all over this damn ship, searching, and no one's seen her!" He paused. "And the bed hadn't been slept in . . . Doctor, I'm worried that . . . that something has happened to her."

"That something has happened to her? Or is it that she may have ..."

Anthony covered his mouth with a hand, spoke through his splayed fingers. "I don't even want to think it."

Swayze frowned. "She did seem a little blue at dinner ... I was seated a few tables away from you."

"Doctor, I'm afraid . . . she was drinking."

Alarm flared in the doctor's eyes. "Mixing alcohol with her medication?"

"Just wine. I didn't say anything to her about it, because I know it relaxes her . . . oh, hell, I blame myself for this ..."

Swayze sighed. "Mr. Vane, there's not much you can do right now, other than return to your room, and try to remain calm."

"That's easily said . . ."

"In the meantime, I'll contact the ship's security. Just try not to worry. She isn't the first person to get lost on this ship. I'm sure she'll turn up."

Keeping a dejected expression going, should he be seen, Anthony strolled along the deck, making his way to his stateroom. It was nearly five in the morning and he paused at the rail, not far from where he'd pitched his wife into the sea; he took in the first purple-pink rays of a magnificent sunrise appearing on the ocean's horizon as the Fantasy slowly cruised into Nassau Harbor, heading for Prince George Wharf.

In the stateroom, Anthony got out of his evening clothes, put on a pair of silk pajamas, climbed into the king size bed and fell fast asleep, dreaming of wealth, no story really, just lots of pretty women and nice things and so very much money.

Around nine, the phone by his bedside rang him awake.

Startled, as if a long-dormant conscience had stirred, he sat up, rubbed his face with the heels of his hands and grabbed the phone before it could ring for a fourth irritating time.

"Hello," he answered thickly.

"Mr. Vane?" a husky voice said.

"Yes."

"This is Jake Lausen." The voice had a Brooklyn tinge. "Chief of ship's security."

"I'm relieved to hear from you, Mr. Lausen—you've found my wife?"

"I'm afraid she hasn't turned up." The voice paused.

"Could you come to my office?"

"Certainly. Where and when, sir?"

"On the Verandah Deck. Would now be convenient?"

"I'll be there in half an hour, if that's all right," Vane told him. "I've been up all night with worry."

"I could see that. Half an hour, Mr. Vane." The phone clicked dead.

In the shower, Anthony mentally rehearsed. He shouldn't appear too distraught—overplaying could raise suspicion; but he had to appear distressed enough, as underplaying could make him seem cold. This needed to be a suicide, otherwise he was the chief suspect—really, the only suspect. He toweled off, blow-dried his hair and applied gel, shaved and splashed on Polo cologne, trying on various faces of concern and sorrow in the mirror. When he stepped from his stateroom, dressed in Armani head to toe, he felt confident he could strike the right tone.

The security office, located next to the radio room on the Verandah Deck, was tiny and messy, files and papers littering the small desk. That put him instantly at ease; nothing about this cubbyhole looked very official.

Except for the chief of security, Jake Lausen. The man gave Anthony a bit of a start: short and stocky, balding, thickly mustached, the man's facial features seemed benignly bland, even baby-ish. But his eyes belonged to a grown-up: under mini-mustache slashes of eyebrow, they were cobalt blue and ball-bearing hard.

What if this Lausen character had been one of New York's finest who'd gotten his fill of big city crime and moved to this cushy job? The man could be a real threat, a slumbering beast awakened by the wrong word or gesture, if Anthony didn't watch his step.

Lausen had opened the door for him and was now gesturing toward a gray steel folding chair across from the cluttered desk. "Have a seat, Mr. Vane, would you?"

"Thank you."

"I've already spoken to Dr. Swayze," Lausen said. He perched on the edge of his desk, looking down at Anthony like a huge stone gargoyle from a church rooftop.

"And he filled me in, as regards to your wife's depression. You mind my asking, was this cruise meant to cheer her up, that sort of thing?"

Anthony, shifting in the uncomfortable metal folding chair (was that on purpose?), nodded. "Yes, precisely. And earlier in the evening, she seemed fine, conversing with the other passengers seated with us for dinner. But then, as has been the case of late, her mood shifted, and she simply didn't seem herself. So we took a brief walk on the deck, and then I escorted her back to our room."

"What was her mood?"

"Withdrawn. Quiet. She and I frequently gamble together, but last night she sent me onto the casino by myself. The last thing she said to me was, 'Enjoy yourself, sweetheart.' " Anthony swallowed; touched the thumb and forefinger of one hand to the bridge of his nose, then drew a breath and composed himself. A nicely acted piece of business, he thought to himself.

"When I returned around three in the morning," Anthony continued, "she wasn't there, and the bed hadn't been slept in."

"Not a good sign," Lausen said, looking thoughtful for a moment. "Is there anything else you can tell me?"

Anthony swallowed. "Well," he began hesitantly. "There is something else."

The security man gazed at him with his ball-bearing eyes. "Last year we took this very same cruise, and . . . Margaret threatened to jump overboard." The first part was true, the second a lie.

"Why?"

"... Why?"

A non-smile twitched under Lausen's mustache. "When people threaten to kill themselves, there's usually a reason. What reason did your wife give you, Mr. Vane?"

"I feel . . . awkward discussing this, Mr. Lausen. As if I might be . . . betraying my wife's confidence."

"This situation is a little beyond social niceties, Mr. Vane. Why did your wife threaten to kill herself last year?"

Anthony heaved a sigh. "She was once a very beautiful woman, Mr. Lausen. She still is ... to me. But she was very unhappy with the way her last cosmetic surgery came out, and as you may have suspected, there's something of an age difference between us ... At any rate, her seventieth birthday was fast approaching, and she became . . . despondent."

All of this was true, more or less—except for the threat of suicide. Margaret had been depressed about her fading beauty—and her husband's roving eye.

"Did you get your wife any help?"

"Of course. She's been seeing a psychiatrist, and has been on anti-depressant medication for almost a year. Well, but then, you know that already, from Dr. Swayze ..."

"Yeah. She ever threaten to kill herself again?"

"No. Never."

"Not even last night?"

"No. But ... I shouldn't say."

"By all means, Mr. Vane, 'say' away."

Another sigh. "I thought perhaps that this cruise . . . being as we'd taken it before, and she'd made that threat, walking on the very deck where we strolled last night . . . this cruise had brought all that unpleasantness back to mind."

The small room fell silent, with Lausen staring down at Anthony from his perch. Then the security chief stood up and went around behind the desk and sat.

"Well, your wife isn't on the ship, Mr. Vane. We've done a cabin-to-cabin canvas, and she didn't disembark in Nassau this morning." He paused. "That leaves only one other place she *could be.*"

Anthony hung his head. "Oh, my God," he said softly. His hands were shaking; he hoped Lausen would see that as sorrow, and not the unexpected nervousness Lausen's hard gaze had engendered in him.

"There's a procedure we follow when a passenger turns up missing, Mr. Vane. I'll have to ask you to remain on board today. I'll want to talk to you again later, and sign some missing person's papers."

Anthony nodded solemnly. "I understand."

"I hope I'm wrong," Lausen said. "And that she turns up. Otherwise . . . sorry for your loss, sir."

But he didn't sound very sorry.

"Thank you," Anthony said, as if the expression of condolence had been sincere. "Should you need me, I'll be in our stateroom."

Anthony hated the thought of that—missing the Nassau stop, losing out on a sumptuous meal at Greycliff, the only five-star restaurant in the Bahamas, and a fun-filled evening in the casinos on Paradise Island. But it was a sacrifice he could live with; after all, with Margaret's money he could come back any time he wanted.

He strolled down the narrow corridor, away from

the security office, wondering if Lausen harbored any major suspicions about him. Perhaps that sour demeanor, that terminal cynicism, simply went with the job.

But so what if Lausen did suspect him? That insignificant little bastard couldn't prove anything. There was only one person on earth—one person on this ship—who could.

He went in search of her.

He was beginning to think she'd gotten off the boat already and gone into Nassau for the day, when he spotted her flaming red hair. Cora and her daughter were up on the sun deck. They were in casual attire, the mother in a knit turquoise pants suit, her daughter in a sunny floral-print sundress, next to each other in deck chairs, big straw hats on their heads, big straw handbags at their feet; their slender, shapely figures were almost identical. When the daughter saw him, her face lighted up and she called out to him.

"Oh, Mr. Vane!" She motioned with one hand. "Could you come here?"

"Good morning, ladies," he said as he approached them, rather surprised by this greeting from the younger woman, who'd barely seemed to notice him last night. "Isn't this sun lovely, after that cold wet evening?"

"Could you do me a tremendous favor?" the pretty blonde woman asked.

"Anything."

"You remember my mother—Cora?"

"How could I forget?"

Cora, that minx, looked up at him with a blank expression, as if he were a stranger.

The daughter said, "Would you please keep her company while I run to the gift shop? I need to pick up some suntan lotion before we head into town."

He beamed at her. "I'd be delighted. Simply delighted." Then he smiled at the mother, who looked back at him with an expression as blank as a doll's.

"I'll be only a minute or so," the daughter said, leaving the two behind.

"Take all the time you need, my dear," he responded.

Anthony settled into the vacated deck chair next to Cora, who was staring out at the magnificent view of Nassau which lay before them, a tourist's dream come true.

He leaned toward her. "And how are you today, my love?"

She turned to him. "Do I know you?" she asked.

He half-smiled at her. She was good; so very good. "You don't have to pretend, now. We don't have to be strangers."

The woman shrugged and looked back at the view.

"What are you going to do with the money?"

She looked at him and blinked. "What money?"

He laughed out loud. "Oh, so *that's* how you're going to play it? I told you last night . . . if you agree to keep our little secret, there will be plenty more where that came from. The question is, Cora—will we be business partners, or could we explore a more pleasant option?"

She didn't respond to that, which unnerved him a little. He'd better find out how much her silence was going to cost him.

"What do you want from me, Cora?" he asked quietly. Gently, he placed a hand on her thigh. "There's so much more than money that I can give you ..."

Cora turned back to him and her placid face came suddenly alive. "I want My Very Own Vanity!" she said.

Such poetry in her speech—her own vanity, indeed. She had that ability so many vixens had, to seem at once a woman and yet child-like in her energy, and her greed.

And he found that beguiling; something about her told him she was a kindred spirit, and he hoped they would not be adversaries.

"What specifically can I give you, my love?"

"I want a Cruisin' Car Convertible."

Now that was specific. Wanting a car was more along the lines he'd expected, but a convertible? She was a remarkable lady; young, at any age . . .

"And what else?" He was almost afraid to ask.

"A Malibu Beach House. I *really* want that."

The back of his neck tingled. "Do you have any idea what a house in Malibu costs these days?"

"Ninety-nine ninety-five."

He laughed hollowly. "Maybe when you were in bloomers, a beach house went for ninety-nine thousand. Now it's more like nine million . . . but maybe that wouldn't be out of the question, my love, if we could share it . . ."

She frowned. "I don't *like* to share my toys."

"I'm back, you two!"

Anthony looked up from his deck chair at Cora's daughter, whose smile upended into a frown. "Is everything all right, Mr. Vane? You look . . . strange. I hope Mother behaved herself."

"She does like to get her way," he said pleasantly, standing.

"Yes, she does," the daughter admitted.

"But she's certainly charming company," he said with a smile, nodding at Cora, who was looking off to the right, as if the children splashing in the ship's pool were particularly fascinating.

"I'm glad you're getting along so famously," said the daughter. "Perhaps we'll see you again, Mr. Vane, when we get back to the ship. Come, Mother, it's time to go."

He watched the pair leave, then wandered back to his room, where he sat on the edge of his bed. This Cora was a shrewd one, blackmailing, scheming bitch that she was; there was much to admire in the woman.

What a team they could make. He could love a woman like that; but could he ever trust her?

And could he ever hope to outsmart the likes of her?

In his state room, Anthony basked in self-pity; everyone else was off roaming the bustling, native-filled streets of Nassau, enjoying the beautiful day, eating traditional Bahamian conch fritters and grouper fingers from colorful vendor carts.

The phone rang beside the bed.

"Mr. Vane," the Brooklyn-tinged voice said, "Jake Lausen again."

"Any news, Mr. Lausen?"

"Afraid not. Need you to stop by my office at four this afternoon."

"All right."

"Listen, you don't have to hang around till then. If you want to get off the ship, go into Nassau, take your mind off things, go ahead."

"Well, that's kind of you, Mr. Lausen. I am getting a little stir-crazy. Walking around the town might help calm my nerves; Margaret's disappearance has me at wit's end."

"No problem. Just be back by four."

As he disembarked onto Woodes Rogers Walk, Anthony tried not to seem *too* happy as he strolled along the harbor where sponge boats were docked, bobbing in the water. Now and then a Bahamian woman tried to get him to buy a straw hat or shell, but he ignored them. He passed over the fresh conch, too, because he had a place in mind for lunch.

Nowhere in the world had he ever had a finer meal than those he'd enjoyed, over the years, at Greycliff. Once the summer home of Lady and Lord Dunmore, the elegant but unpretentious restaurant catered to the well-off, from royalty to rock stars, from CEOs to drug dealers. All of their food was magnificent, but his favorite was the well-cooked goose.

Crossing Bay Street, crowded by mid-afternoon with its horse-drawn surreys carrying well-heeled tourists, he quickened his step as he thought about the culinary delights which awaited him just a few blocks away, up steep Blue Hill Road. As he passed Rawson's Square, where tuckered-out travelers sat on quaint wooden benches, he stopped short. Sitting in the shade of a palm tree, with their backs to him, but their identity unmistakable, were Jennifer and Cora.

The daughter seemed somewhat worked up, saying impatiently to her mother, "All right, I'll go back to the store and buy it, even though it's not the right one . . . But you have to *promise* me not to move from this bench."

He couldn't hear what the mother said, but saw her nod her head, yes. Then Jennifer stood up, and hurried across the plaza.

He approached Cora, whipping off his Ray-Bans dramatically. "Well, hello, my love," he said, looming over her. "We meet again."

She ignored him, continuing to mutter to herself.

"What's wrong?" he asked. "Not having a good time?"

"No," she said, scrunching up her face, like a kid talking back to a parent.

This coy act was starting to get to him; she was attractive, but playing cute simply wasn't cute, at her age.

"What's the matter, my love?"

"We couldn't find him."

"Who?"

"Nibbles."

"Nibbles?"

"The right horse."

He couldn't imagine why she was looking for a horse.

"Well, I'm sure he's around somewhere." After all, there were plenty of horses pulling carriages in downtown Nassau. Then he asked, "Where did your lovely daughter go?"

Cora looked at him oddly. "I don't have a daughter."

"Oh, I see." He smiled. "Have a fight, did you?"

She looked away, pouting.

And he made a decision; sudden, but necessary. This woman was too unpredictable, too cunning. Right now he didn't want a lover or need a partner; and he certainly didn't require some blackmailing bitch, however clever and attractive, in his life.

"Have you been up the Queen's Staircase yet?" he asked, working some enthusiasm into his voice. The last thing he wanted to do right now was trudge up some cliff-side stairway. But if it was the last thing *Cora* did, it would be worth the effort. . .

"No."

"It's just a short distance from here. And at the top of the stairs is a fort with all the armaments; it's like stepping into the past. Very romantic."

She considered that. "You mean, like My Very Own Castle?"

"*Our* very own castle," he said, and touched her thigh.

"Oh, take me there. Take me there now!"

Just off East Street, steep steps had been carved into a limestone hill leading to Fort Fincastle. Shaped like a paddle-wheel steamer, the small fortress was built to protect the town from any enemy who landed. Heavy cast-iron cannons pointed out to sea, guns that had never been fired.

Cora climbed briskly, with an enthusiasm and energy a young girl might have envied. What a handful she was! What a pity she had to go . . .

Halfway up the steps Anthony halted. "Let me rest," he said, wiping sweat from his brow, "catch my breath a second." He couldn't believe that the older woman wasn't even breathing hard.

"Well, okay, but not for long." She was standing one step ahead of him. "I want to see the castle."

Two teenagers, most likely brother and sister, squeezed around them on the steps, raced each other to the top, soon disappearing from view.

Then they were alone on the stairs.

He felt a pang of regret; what a beautiful relationship he might have had with such a beautiful, vibrant and oh so cagey a woman . . .

"Okay, I'm ready," he said and they continued the climb, with her in the lead and him just behind. As they neared the top, he reached out and gave her arm a quick, vicious tug, side-stepping as she fell backward past him, cascading down the limestone steps, leaving red impressions as she went.

He didn't stick around to watch her tumble all the way down, but turned, wanting to remove himself from the scene and let someone else discover the body, and bolted to the top.

And bumped into a man beginning to descend.

A baby-faced, mustached man named Jake Lausen.

"Well, Mr. Vane," Lausen said, "it doesn't look like you're having a very relaxing cruise, now, does it?"

Lausen was again perched on the edge of his desk, with Anthony seated before him in the hard, cold folding chair.

"Disaster seems to follow you, Mr. Vane, wherever you go."

Anthony avoided the security chiefs glare. "I've told you a dozen times, it was an accident," he said. "I was taking Cora—Mrs. Hazen—to see the fort and she lost her footing, and slipped on the stairs."

"Problem with that story," Lausen said, "is I saw you give the gal *a yank,* to help her along."

Anthony said nothing.

Lausen sighed. "Of course, I'm just a little old eyewitness. I'm sure the victim herself will have her own opinion of exactly what happened."

Anthony looked at him sharply.

"That's right," Lausen smiled nastily, "she's got some broken bones, some bumps, some scratches, a concussion. But she's a tough old gal. Dr. Swayze will be bringing her here in a few minutes to give a statement."

Anthony sat forward, gesturing frantically. "It was an accident, I tell you. I mean, maybe it was *me* who slipped on the steps, and I grabbed her to catch my balance ..."

"Again, let's see what Mrs. Hazen thinks—and I'm hoping she'll have some idea of what your motive might've been. After all, I can understand why you tossed your rich wife over the rail ..."

"That was uncalled for."

"It sure as hell as was."

Anthony scowled at the smug son of a bitch. "What were you doing there, anyway, Lausen?"

"When I saw you head up the stairs, I couldn't follow, since I was in a car," Lausen said flatly. "I took the drive up to the top . . . see, my men and me have been keeping you in our sights ever since you reported your wife missing, and saw you hookin' up with this Hazen woman. It's gonna be real interesting findin' how she's involved—but I'm sure she'll be willing to fill us in, now that you've just tried to kill her."

There was a sharp knock at the door, and Lausen said, "Come on in."

The door opened and Cora Hazen came slowly in, on crutches, one arm in a cast, a bandage wrapped around her head as if she had a big toothache. Dr. Swayze followed right behind her.

Anthony groaned at the sight of her and lowered his gaze and shook his head.

"Mrs. Hazen," Lausen said gently, "how are you

feeling?"

"Awful!" she snapped. "Just awful. *Somebody* pushed me down some stairs."

"All right, all right," Anthony blurted, "I waive my rights. I pushed her. I pushed the silly bitch!"

"And your wife?" Lausen asked.

"Ask Cora Hazen—she was there. She saw me throw Margaret over the side. She . . . she saw it all."

Lausen smiled, gestured to Anthony. "Mrs. Hazen, is there anything you'd like to tell us about this man?"

Cora looked sideways at the doctor, then at Lausen, and finally at Vane. "I've never seen him before in my life!" she said. "But he is a nice-looking gentleman."

"Thank you, Mrs. Hazen," Lausen said. "That'll be all for now."

And when they'd gone, Lausen told Anthony.

"Alzheimer's?" Anthony asked.

And Anthony began to laugh, laughter that turned to tears as he buried his face in hands, wishing he could forget.

That night, on deck, standing at the rail, Jennifer Kafer and Dr. Thomas Swayze looked out at the gently rolling ocean painted ivory by moonlight.

"You've been wonderful about Mother," she said to him. She wore a blue evening gown and he wore his dress uniform. Her arm was hooked in the crook of his.

"Keeping her in the infirmary, under constant watch," he said, "is a precaution I felt needed taking."

"I hate to say this, but it is nice to have some time

away from her, alone ... I mean, I love her, and as you said, I feel lucky that this disease has taken only her memory, not turned her mean or ugly."

"You can have many wonderful moments with your mother . . . worth remembering."

"Even if she can't," Jennifer said, with sad, wry smile.

"You know what you need?"

"What do you prescribe, doctor?"

"You need some memories of your own ..." And he kissed her, and she kissed back; it was just a shipboard romance, of course, but it would be fun for both of them, to look back on in their old age.

Copyright Information

A Look At:
An Eliot Ness Mystery Omnibus

A FAST-PACED, ONE-TWO PUNCH OF CRIME AND DROP DEAD SUSPENSE.

Legendary lawman Eliot Ness goes solo… In 1929, Eliot Ness put away Al Scarface Capone and became the biggest living legend this side of law and order. Now it's 1935. With The Untouchables and Prohibition behind him and the Great Depression falling darkly across the nation, Ness arrives in Cleveland to straighten out a crooked city.

An anonymous ring of bent cops is dealing in vice, graft, gambling and racketeering, over lorded by a mysterious top cop known as the outside chief. But between corrupt politicians, jealous colleagues, a parasitic reporter and two blondes with nothing in common, Ness has big troubles pulling the sheets off the bed of blue vipers.

"For anybody who loves crime novels, Max Allen Collins is the gold standard."

An Eliot Ness Mystery Omnibus includes: Dark City, Butcher's Dozen, Bullet Proof and Murder by The Numbers.

AVAILABLE NOW

About the Authors

MAX ALLAN COLLINS was named a Grand Master in 2017 by the Mystery Writers of America. He is a three-time winner of thc Private Eye Writers of America "Shamus" award, receiving the PWA "Eye" for Life Achievement (2006) and their "Hammer" award for making a major contribution to the private eye genre with the Nathan Heller saga (2012).

His graphic novel Road to Perdition (1998) became the Academy Award-winning Tom Hanks film, followed by prose sequels and several graphic novels. His other comics credits include the syndicated strip "Dick Tracy"; "Batman"; and his own "Ms. Tree" and "Wild Dog."

His innovative Quarry novels were adapted as a 2016 TV series by Cinemax. His other suspense series include Eliot Ness, Krista Larson, Reeder and Rogers, and the

"Disaster" novels. He has completed twelve "Mike Hammer" novels begun by the late Mickey Spillane; his audio novel, Mike Hammer: The Little Death with Stacy Keach, won a 2011 Audie.

For five years, he was sole licensing writer for TV's CSI: Crime Scene Investigation (and its spin-offs), writing best-selling novels, graphic novels, and video games. His tie-in books have appeared on the USA TODAY and New York Times bestseller lists, including Saving Private Ryan, Air Force One, and American Gangster.

Collins has written and directed four features and two documentaries, including the Lifetime movie "Mommy" (1996) and "Mike Hammer's Mickey Spillane" (1998); he scripted "The Expert," a 1995 HBO World Premiere and "The Last Lullaby" (2009) from his novel The Last Quarry. His Edgar-nominated play "Eliot Ness: An Untouchable Life" (2004) became a PBS special, and he has co-authored (with A. Brad Schwartz) two non-fiction books on Ness, Scarface and the Untouchable (2018) and Eliot Ness and the Mad Butcher (2020).

Collins and his wife, writer Barbara Collins, live in Iowa; as "Barbara Allan," they have collaborated on sixteen novels, including the "Trash 'n' Treasures" mysteries, Antiques Flee Market (2008) winning the Romantic Times Best Humorous Mystery Novel award of 2009. Their son Nathan has translated numerous novels into English from Japanese, as well as video games and manga.

*****

BARBARA COLLINS made her entrance into the mystery field as a highly respected short story writer with appearances in over a dozen top anthologies, including Murder Most Delicious, Women on the Edge, Deadly Housewives and the best-selling Cat Crimes series. She was the co-editor of (and a contributor to) the best-selling anthology Lethal Ladies, and her stories were selected for inclusion in the first three volumes of The Year's 25 Finest Crime and Mystery Stories.

As "Barbara Allan," she and her husband Max Allan Collins write the long-running "Trash 'n' Treasures" mystery series. Their Antiques Flee Market (2008) won the Romantic Times "Best Humorous Mystery Novel" award of 2009. They have also appeared under their joint byline in Ellery Queen's Mystery Magazine.

The Collins's first novel together, the Baby Boomer thriller Regeneration, was a paperback bestseller; their second collaborative novel, Bombshell – in which Marilyn Monroe saves the world from World War III – was published in hardcover to excellent reviews. Both are back in print from Thomas & Mercer under their "Barbara Allan" byline.

Two acclaimed hardcover collections of Barbara's work have been published – Too Many Tomcats and (with her husband) Murder - His and Hers, with a follow-up, Suspense – His and Hers – coming from

Wolfpack, who are bringing out the previous collections as well.

Barbara also has been the production manager and/or line producer on several of Max's independent film projects, including Mommy (1995), Mommy's Day (1997), Real Time: Siege at Lucas Street Market (2001) and Eliot Ness: An Untouchable Life (2005).

The writing duo lives in their native Muscatine, Iowa. Their son, Nathan, is a Japanese-to-English translator with numerous books, manga and video games to his credit. Barb divides her time between writing and providing Day Care for her two grand-childen, Sam and Lucy.

Made in the USA
Monee, IL
03 September 2021